Hero Society

Night

Jessica Florence

Jessica Florence© 2018

Editing by Librum Artis Editorial Services

Proofreading by Judy's Proofreading

Cover by Sarah Hansen, Okay Creations©

Prologue

Esme

2007

"Please, Eli, let me heal you," I begged, my eyes unable to cry the tears I wanted to shed.

My twin brother shook his head, tubes and wires attached everywhere on his body as he lay in the hospital bed.

"No." His voice was low, but it still held that same annoying brother tone he always used when he was not budging on an issue.

"I don't care about me—I'd rather live a shorter life with you being my brother than be without you."

We'd had this conversation over and over since he became sick. I had the ability to heal him, so he wouldn't die from the leukemia that was eating away at his body. We'd been through this before over the years, but this time there was no coming back.

My fraternal twin, with the same reddish-brown hair and hazel-green eyes as me, was going to die soon. Maybe today, maybe tomorrow, maybe over the upcoming weekend. The fact was I was going to lose him, and even though I could save him, he wouldn't let me. And if I did it without his permission, he would never forgive me.

His weak fingers gripped my arm that rested on his, rubbing slightly over the faint gold line that ran over my vein. My lifeline.

"You're worth it." I wanted to cry, I wanted to throw things, I just wanted him to not choose death.

"You're going to live the life I never could. You're going to fall in love, and it'll be the type of love that you've always dreamed of—the love that legends are made of. You're going to do so many great things in your life, Esme, and if I let you heal me, I could be taking that away from you. My fate was sealed a long time ago. You still have control over your destiny."

I heard his words, but I still was in denial.

"Just tell my future nieces about their uncle, Eli, and how cool he was, okay?" He laughed, and it was my turn to shake my head...this was Eli, always trying to be the light in any darkness.

"I'm going to tell them about that one time when we were at the pool and you decided it would be funny to jump from the diving board and pull your pants down, showing everyone your junk." We were both laughing then, even though his eyes started to glisten with emotion.

"Be good to Mom and Dad, too," he directed, and I nodded. Mom and Dad had been going through a divorce when leukemia decided it was going to take Eli. They'd been having a hard time before, and now they were both struggling to hold on at all.

"You gotta find Lola and play fetch with her until I get there, all right?"

Our family dog had died last year, and I prayed that dog heaven and people heaven met so they could be together until we were able to join him.

He nodded, and the tears started to roll down his cheeks.

"Hey, you're my tough big brother. You're not supposed to be the one to cry," I choked out, and he snorted.

"Two minutes older and suddenly I'm the responsible one."

"You've always been the responsible one," I reminded him. His grip pulled me closer, and I knew what he wanted.

We've always had that connection that twins do. What he felt, I felt—and right now he was scared.

I crawled into the small space next to his body on the bed, and he wrapped his arm around my shoulder, the other reaching to hold my hand.

"I'm choosing to let you live, Esme." His voice broke, barely holding onto his emotions.

"You've been with me since the beginning, brother, and you'll be with me till the end," I whispered to his chest, knowing by the bond between us that his thread was about to be cut.

"Always with you, till the very end, Esme. Live hard, love strong, and when you're feeling lost, I'll be your light when the darkness comes." His breath was soft, and then I felt it.

The bond was shattered, and my brother sighed, his arm falling from my shoulder.

To have the power to heal, only to draw nearer to death with every use: a curse, not a gift, if I couldn't even save the ones I loved the most.

Chapter One

Present Day

Esme

"Happy birthday, Eli."

I stared at the red velvet cupcake that had a blue candle lit on top. Next to it was another lit cupcake—funfetti flavor—for me. I never cared for red velvet that much, but it was Eli's favorite, so I endured.

I still celebrated our birthday together.

I blew out his candle first, wishing he was happy wherever he was in the afterlife he chose, and then blew out mine, wishing the same thing I wished for every year.

True love, and for there to be no more pain in the world.

Both were pretty unattainable wishes, but I still closed my eyes and told the universe that's what I wanted.

I inhaled my funfetti cupcake then went about getting my scrubs on and my hair up into a messy bun on top of my head. Most women my age would be going out at this hour, dressed to slay the hearts of men, and have wild, drunken sex all night.

Me? I was heading into the night shift at the hospital. It paid more, and it made me feel like I was doing something positive, even though the world was going to hell in a handbasket. Ever since that night when the crazy pastor gave people with powers a hallucinogen, there was a civil war in the streets. A quiet one for now, but still it wouldn't be quiet for long.

I stood in the small bathroom of my one-bedroom apartment looking at my hot mess of a reflection.

"Live hard and love strong, Esme. Be happy." I pinched my cheeks to add some color to them, reminding myself that I needed to get out more, see the sun. I'd been doing nothing but working my ass off at the hospital, and had added part-time nurse duty at the Hero Society headquarters when they needed me. Phillip called to tell me that the vials of the blood samples I'd taken from each of them had been broken, so I'd need to do another set soon. I'd wanted to examine them for any anomalies, diseases, and vulnerabilities. I'd been helping other people with powers since I became a nurse, and now I would be helping the heroes that risked their lives to save others.

Like me.

I smiled to myself, and then walked into the living room, grabbing my coat and shoes.

My eyes caught a shiny gold light on my arm, and I cursed. I'd almost forgotten to cover up my thread.

I rushed back into the bathroom and sat on the toilet lid while I covered up the gold line that was now half the size of my forearm with makeup.

My life thread: a golden shimmer in my vein that ran down the middle of my left arm and had appeared on my sixteenth birthday.

After saving a squirrel our dog had caught, I realized I could heal the hurt.

Eli and I discovered that every time I used my power to heal, the thin gold line would get shorter. Usually not a lot, but it was still nerve-racking, so we threw ourselves into every bit of research we could find. Nothing was making sense until we read about the Fates: three creatures of destiny and life. One sister spun the thread of someone's life, the second sister determined how long they lived, and the final sister cut the thread, deciding how they died. The gods had golden blood called ichor in their bodies, so their thread could not be cut.

We were sold on the notion that every time I used my powers, I inched closer to death, potentially chopping years off my life with every heal. Whatever the truth was, deep down we both knew that when that golden line disappeared, things would not be good.

Once the gold was covered and my arm appeared normal, I bundled up to face the snow that had started falling outside, grabbed the red velvet cupcake to eat on the way, and walked out the door.

The rent was stupid for such a tiny apartment, but it was close to the hospital. I could walk to work and be there in the event of an emergency.

If I couldn't save everyone with my powers, then I wanted to save as many as I could the good old-fashioned way—being a nurse.

The cupcake was gone by the time I walked the five minutes to work.

The hospital seemed quiet tonight, but that didn't mean anything. It was 11:00 p.m. on a Friday. Anything could happen.

I put my coat in my locker and went to the nurses' station in the ER. Tammy, the second-shift nurse, was just closing out her paperwork when I joined her.

"Have fun." The poor girl seemed tired as hell, almost sighing the words.

"Get some sleep." I patted her on the shoulder as she exited the station.

I sat in the wobbly desk chair that needed to be replaced.

Ten minutes after reading through Tammy's notes, I felt his presence, his dark energy sending a chill through me.

"Good evening, Dr. Dorian. Is there anything I can help you with?" My monotone voice held no happiness to see the prized doctor of the hospital.

"You doing your job is a good start." He spoke in the same deadpan tone as I had.

My head tilted up to see his look of disdain before he turned his eyes toward the charts in his hands.

I hated it when he looked at me like that, like I was a child who liked playing nurse on her parents' living room floor.

I'd worked hard to get where I was today, and when he gave me that face, I was tempted to throw it all away for the opportunity to smack his handsome face.

"If you keep staring at me like that, you're going to have a coronary over there." Dr. Dorian turned to walk away after setting his charts down at the nurses' station. He strutted around here like he was better than everyone, and I couldn't wait for the day someone knocked him off his high horse.

"What I wouldn't give for a piece of that man. I bet he fucks like a savage in bed after being all uptight and reserved at the hospital all day." I turned to see my coworker and friend Melissa Ann eyeing Dorian's retreating form.

"Are you kidding? That man would probably never stoop low enough to sleep with someone. I think he's asexual," I commented and began reading over my next patient to visit. But Melissa wasn't done with this topic.

"I'm a married woman with one toddler and a baby on the way. Let me daydream about the good doctor being a beast in the supply closet. If you were more the adventurous type, I'd tell you to hit that between shifts, and then you could go back to spitting at each other." Melissa had just found out last month that she was pregnant, and was thrilled, despite her fantasies of Dorian.

I'd had those dreams, too, when I first moved to Seahill in search of a fresh start, hoping to live out the rest of my short life living freely and falling in love.

For the first week, I thought maybe he could have been the one to help this little mouse of a girl come out of her shell and experience life at its fullest. But he shot me down with a raised eyebrow and a sneer.

I was too innocent and not worth a quick fuck in the on-call rooms.

It stung, but I didn't let him see that. Ever since then, we'd engaged in a cold war. He pushed my buttons, and I ignored him.

"Never in a million years," I told her as I spared a glance to the doctor as he stood in front of a room, looking over their history. His head snapped up, and his gaze collided with mine. His eyes narrowed, as if he knew from afar that I wanted to stick my tongue out at him. Then those eyes flared with something I couldn't read, and he disappeared inside the patient's room.

"Girl, deny it all you want, but this tension you two have for each other is going to come to a

head one day and I suggest you use it in the way the good Lord intended us to utilize that passion, instead of stabbing him with your chart pen."
Melissa went back to her work, but I stayed rooted, staring at the space where Dorian had been.

I was still voting for smacking him on his scruffy jaw over screwing him between patients.

Chapter Two

Esme

"Happy birthday!"

There was a small crowd gathered in the breakroom around a cake when I shuffled in for my "lunch" break at 3:30 a.m.

"Thanks, guys." I smiled and leaned over to blow out the candle.

"Wish for something different," Melissa whispered, and I looked up at her to see her sweet, beaming smile. She knew I always wished for the same thing. My gaze moved back to the cake in front of me, and I thought about making a new one. Just for this cake.

I closed my eyes and blew it out.

I wished for passion.

True love may not be out there for me in the time I had left, but if I could find an all-consuming passion, that would be close enough for me.

All six of the people in the room cheered then waited for their piece of cake as soon as I was done. Melissa handed me the first slice, and I sat on the small couch against the wall.

Our breakroom was nice as far as hospitals went—it had a microwave, a fridge, sink, and three tables with four chairs each. There was a comfy couch and a decent-sized TV in the corner. Simple but nice. Seahill Hospital was one of the top facilities in the world and the doctors here were rock stars of the medical community, so in shared facilities like this, there were some perks.

That first bite of cake was heavenly. Melissa Ann knew how to bake a great cake. I groaned in appreciation, and then *he* appeared as if notified by the universe that this was the right moment to mess with me.

"Moaning like a whore in church over cake. Classy, Esme."

I looked at the devil sitting next to me and stared right back into his brown eyes as I brought another big piece to my mouth, making a grand show of how much I enjoyed Melissa Ann's handiwork.

"No wonder you can't find a man to take the edge off. Your moaning and writhing over cake scares them away." Dorian smirked, and I rolled my eyes.

"No man can compare to the heavenly taste of cake." I licked the icing off my fork and went back to the rest of my slice for more.

He chuckled and then we were silent. He was sitting so close that I could feel his body heat.

"Is there a reason you're here?" I blurted out. He was ruining my happy moment in one of the only breaks I'd probably get for the rest of the night.

"I'm quite partial to this couch," he replied while looking at his watch. *Yes, have some other place you have to be, please.*

I'm guessing my thoughts were visible on my face because he got more comfortable on his cushion, hands going behind his head for support.

Ass.

"Okay, well, you're ruining my happy space, so go save the world, Dorian." I tried to shoo him away, and he caught the hand that was doing the shooing and studied the icing-covered fork gripped in my fist.

He wouldn't.

His eyes met mine as he leaned in toward my hand and wrapped his lips around my fork.

My tummy fluttered at the sight of his mouth savoring the icing, but then my head shut down the flutter and replaced it with annoyance.

"Thanks for the herpes," I hissed and jerked my fork away, looking around, hoping no one noticed what was happening over here. I'd never hear the end of it. Thankfully only Melissa Ann was watching, giving me the side-eye while talking to another nurse.

"They all know I don't fuck where I work. Your sweet reputation isn't tarnished." It's been a while since he's messed with me about sex stuff, so I guess it shouldn't be a surprise that he would bring that one back into rotation for a special occasion like my birthday. He usually kept with the incompetence lines.

"You can go now."

I was usually an easy, down-to-earth woman, but this man dragged something nasty out of me every time. He hadn't earned my niceness.

"I'm curious if your new friends know how dismissive you are to your coworkers. They might change their mind if they did." He looked like the cat who ate the canary.

I was stunned by his words since they suggested he knew I was now working with the Hero Society, but my reaction was what he wanted.

"I'm not dismissive to anyone but you, and you clearly aren't broken up by it." I gazed down at my cake, wanting to eat it, but didn't want to use the contaminated fork or go bother Melissa Ann for a new one.

"Awesome, you've officially ruined my birthday cake. Great job, Dorian." I sighed and stood to leave, repeating to myself that I wasn't going to let him get to me.

I had patients I needed to go check on, anyway. After tossing my leftover cake in the trash, then hugging Melissa Ann for the surprise, I left the room to get back to work.

The hospital was quiet as I walked down the hallway to the ER. Suddenly hands grabbed me, yanking my body into a room. The door snapped shut behind me, and I drew in a breath to scream, but whoever grabbed me pressed their lips to mine.

My eyes were wide as I took in the dark hair and brown eyes in front of me.

Not just anyone was pressed against me with his lips to mine.

It was Dorian.

His hands relaxed their grip on my body, one sliding down my arm to rest against my hip while the other cupped my jaw, trying to open me up, stroking gently.

My lips parted in shock, my brain urging me to tell him to get the fuck off me, but then his teeth nipped my lower lip before his tongue flicked it afterwards, and my body melted, kissing him back.

My chest arched against his body as his hot mouth fucked mine. He tasted like icing and pure desire, making my hands move to his neck, pulling him into me more. He growled, and I moaned at the sound. Oh God, he was sin incarnate. Dorian knew what he was doing, and he was currently possessing my body through his lips.

Then he pulled back, his eyes smug as he took in my wet lips, blushed cheeks, and hooded eyes.

"Best present I could give you, other than my cock. Enjoy the memories."

It was like he dumped a giant bucket of ice-cold water over my head. This was a—no, I couldn't even come up with what the hell this was.

In my anger, I gripped the small hairs at the back of his neck, enjoying his snarl from the pain it caused.

His eyes flashed with revenge but then smoldered into something different, something that made me feel like he was about to kiss me again and this time not stop.

I let go of his neck and pushed him back, ready to get out of the supply closet he'd dragged me into.

His face and body posture were still rigid like a man on edge, one that was close to lunging for me. Nope. Fuck that.

"Thanks for the memories. Now I definitely remember why I hate you." I opened the door and walked away with as much cool composure as I could. I heard the door behind me open and close hard, but he didn't come after me.

Once I got home I would let myself think about what just happened, but right now I had to focus on my job. Especially when two men came in via ambulance from a bad car accident.

I had people who needed me, and I could help them, one way or another.

Chapter Three

Dorian

She thinks she won that round in the supply closet.

But all she's done is show me that the little mouse has a backbone, and that has made me curious.

I'd ventured into the breakroom knowing they'd have some party for her birthday, and I knew it would annoy her for me to be there. Something about getting her to let go of the good-girl mask made the sharp edges in my mind dull. She normally just ignores me, which is better for the both of us, if I'm to be honest.

I'd never looked at her as anything more than a nuisance: a woman gifted by the gods, yet didn't use her power. I knew the moment she walked up to talk to me on her first day that there was something different about her. That stench of life and death in one body...the Fates had blessed her with that gift.

But they were also cruel, and I'd no doubt that she would eventually give all her life away to save someone. She was pure good, through and through.

Which is why I'd left her alone. Her petite, elven-like face and frame didn't call to me as a man. I'd break her in two. And her power, combined with the innocence inside her, didn't make me crave her for my side of the war. It wasn't worth the effort to try to keep out of the hands of the Hero Society. She would help them as best as she could, but it would either kill her in the end, or she wouldn't affect anything. So, I've let her be, allowing her to play nurse and living out her trivial life.

Until she tried to shoo me away, like I was a fly begging for cake. Her eyes had dilated, and her lips had parted as I licked her fork, and my mind conjured an image of licking that icing off her creamy skin instead.

The desire to taste her drove me wild, and her words made me chase after her, compelled to savor that fight on her tongue.

Now she's shown me that she can play my game without yielding.

I'm curious, and when you've lived as long as I have, things don't make you curious anymore.

There was still some time—a few weeks before my army would be ready. I wondered how long it would take to bend her to me, to use her body and break in her mind.

For the last few days, following our kiss, she wouldn't look at me unless we were in front of a patient together. She was trying to move on and forget that her body trembled at my touch, that she moaned into my breath, and her hands had pulled me closer. There was no forgetting that.

"I can feel you staring at me."

She was checking the unconscious patient's vitals while I administered his medication. Technically she could have done this all on her own, but I thought tagging along would aggravate her and maybe she would show me her backbone again.

"I'm wondering what noises you make when you come," I remarked and smirked as her cheeks grew red.

She looked tired today. Her hair was up in that disaster she called a messy bun, her scrubs were wrinkled, and her face looked pale. Well, paler. Even the freckles that covered her face looked dull.

She sighed and finished writing a note in her chart.

"I don't have time for this, Dorian. Can you go back to being an asshole, thinking I'm an incompetent nurse, and stop with the innuendo?" A plea. I sneered hearing it. Where was the feisty woman who shooed me away, who gripped my hair and made my cock hard?

"Why are you so tired?" I demanded, not liking it one bit that she wasn't up for playing with me. She peered at me with an expression that said it was none of my business. True, but for some reason I was making my business.

"I just have a lot going on, and you are making it worse," she told me and then walked out the door. If I wanted to, I could chase her down and demand she tell me what the problem was, but I stopped myself.

I had a plan, and I was so close I could finally feel victory in my grasp.

After looking around and seeing no one else was there, I flashed to one of my many homes.

This one in particular housed my weapons—men and women I'd found in the chaos of their lives and easily won over with promises of a life without fear for people like them. They could

27

be who they wanted to be without anyone saying otherwise. Humans were beneath them. Beneath me.

My hands clenched at the thought of how beneath me they were.

Me, the sole survivor of the demigods.

That familiar taste of anger and bitterness crept over my tongue. I swallowed it down, feeling it burn as it moved throughout my body.

Those with powers that had been gifted by the gods were just that—gifted. They had no blood of the gods running through their veins; they were chosen.

The gods cared so much about the humans that they made sure they could protect them after they perished.

But their own children were left for dead, murdered by each other's hands and the hands of their parents.

The only reason I survived was because I had given myself a toxin that would make me appear dead. I woke up days later to see that every last one of the demigods had been slain.

I'd been good once, a healer for man, and always doing the work of my father, Apollo, god of the sun, music, medicine, and prophecy. He was an eclectic bastard. But still I yearned for his approval, using my powers to help mankind until the gods turned on us, deeming all demigods expendable. Even the good ones, like I was.

I watched with my own eyes as they chose Draco to be their leader of heroes.

I watched as they gave him their power and burned into his back with their blood searing tattoos of their godly symbols into his skin.

The chosen one. Chosen over their own children.

I was angry and jealous, and I let it all fester. My hatred for Draco grew, and I sought to destroy him, only to find out he was immortal. Even demigods would die eventually.

So, I drafted my plan: become immortal, stop Draco from succeeding in his mission, and let mankind fall to their own chaos.

The first part was easy. I'd found immortality through the blood of the gifted. The other two had been my obstacle all these years.

But I was almost there. I'd slain those Draco had found if he didn't do it himself.

When man was given the power of the gods, they tended to want to use that power for their needs. I couldn't fault them for that. Draco did, though. And still his Hero Society forgives him for killing people like them who he deemed unfit.

I would have let them loose, and soon I will.

His blood has been the key all along.

By mixing Draco's blood with others that have the power genes in the DNA, the powers have kept in their new hosts. Finally, I will have my revenge.

Chapter Four

Esme

"Thanks for inviting me out. I haven't had a girls' night since...well, a very long time," I told the three women that were sitting around a table with me at Club V. The music was pumping, and the drinks were flowing.

"Sometimes we just need to get away from all the testosterone in headquarters," Rose said with a grin, and I smiled back. She and I were kindred spirits, sweet, but underneath lay a warrior's heart. I'd yet to find mine, but I could feel the beast inside me rumbling. Lilith and Echo nodded, and I held out my shot for a toast. They raised their lemon drops, and I looked into their eyes.

"Here's to bringing some more tits into the Hero Society!" I laughed and downed my drink. Gross. Drinking was not my thing, but I was taking one for the team tonight.

They all cheered and drank their shots in unison.

I was tired from working the past few days without too much sleep, but I was ready to enjoy my night with the girls. It made my day when Rose suggested we all go out.

Echo looked different tonight—a positive change I'd seen in her since she caught Dr. Nathan. The guy had always creeped me out, I tried to stay away from that section of the hospital if I could. She seemed freer, like she could be happy for once, and I was glad.

Lilith was the woman I always wished I could be. Brazen, smart, and totally confident. Whatever she wanted, she went for. She didn't hold back. She also had a gift for making any woman around her feel beautiful, which I completely appreciated.

Everyone looked beautiful tonight. Rose was wearing a pretty sweater dress and knee-high boots. Echo wore her signature look of black jeans, boots, and a shirt with the leather jacket, but it still looked hot on her. Always did. Lilith was wearing boots as well, joined with high-waisted shorts and a crop top. It was snowing outside, and seemed impervious to the cold.

I was wearing my only pair of skinny jeans, with black boots and a skintight sweater that came up to my collarbone but then dipped around my neck and plunged to my lower back. I bought it years ago, thinking I'd be brave and wear it out on a date, but I hadn't been on a date since before that purchase. That was a depressing thought.

"I miss sex." I voiced my thoughts, and the girls looked at me, puzzled expressions on their faces.

"When was the last time you got some?" Lilith asked, and the others waited for my answer.

My head dropped to the table in shame as I told them.

"One year, eight months, and sixteen days."

All three of them groaned, and Rose reached over to rub my back in comfort.

"I was a virgin until Draco," she said, and I looked up in surprise. I wouldn't have guessed that. She kept going with her story, explaining that with her powers, she just didn't trust anyone until him. He was the only one she wanted, and he didn't let her down. Every time they were around each other it was like seeing two halves of a soul. They were magnetic.

Lilith gave me her story next, then Echo. I felt bad having brought up that I hadn't had sex in a while, when each of these ladies until recently had never had sex or had horrible experiences beforehand.

"I always wanted that kind of love you read in old legends, the kind of love that never dies. So, I kissed a bunch of frogs, and all I got was lots of heartache and disappointment. I've just been working too much to even attempt something now." I ordered another shot and quickly swallowed it down once it hit the table.

"You should get drunk and have wild sex tonight," Echo commented, and Lilith looked at her like she just solved the mystery of life. Her squeal was loud, and she clapped her hands together in excitement.

"Yes! Tonight's mission: get Esme drunk so she lets that cute-girl layer melt off and the sexy siren come out to play!" Her excitement was making me smile, and I wished I could do as she said, but I still had reservations. I wasn't a one-night type of girl.

"Honestly, with everything going on in the world, you might as well do what you want and live it up. Who knows when it will be our last day?" Rose shrugged and ordered another drink for herself. I studied her, soaking in her words because they were the words I tried to live by since my brother died. I had been living my life to a point, but I was still hiding. I had wished moments before that I could be like Lilith, because she just did what she wanted that made her happy—but now was my time.

"Screw it. Live hard, love strong. Let's do this!"

We drank, we laughed, and let whatever worries we had go for one short night.

Lilith convinced me to go into her favorite bird cage and dance my heart out. I did it, and I felt the opposite of caged—I felt free.

Rose was all giggly as she made Echo dance with her to a famous pop song about being twenty-two. Echo smiled and let go, which was hard for her, though alcohol probably helped. It was sure as shit helping me let my good girl go, and allow whatever hot mess I was inside out to have some fun. I wasn't even thinking about men as I danced to the beat, purely enjoying myself.

I left the cage for a bathroom break, and when I came back, the girls were dancing together. I watched them and felt the bonds of sisterhood grow between us. I was glad I decided to join them, not just because of their cause to help people, but because they were a family, and one I wanted to be a part of.

My hips started swaying to the beat as I moved toward them, but then hands loosely wrapped themselves around my hips and pulled me back against a hard torso. I closed my eyes, feeling myself relax, letting my hands reach up to touch the person behind me. I didn't care who I was with, but I knew for certain that I was indeed dancing with a man. And if my hands were feeling things correctly, a man with a fantastic body.

His hips moved with mine, grinding in unison as if there were no clothes between us. I hadn't really considered getting laid, even though the girls had decided it was going to be my goal for the night, but I was thinking about it now.

Whoever I was dancing with was sexy as hell, and the way he moved against me, his hand keeping me flush to his body was turning me on like nothing else. A memory flashed in my head of the last time I was turned on this much, and I knew if I hadn't been completely drunk I would have realized who this was much sooner. There was only one person who made me feel like this.

"What are you doing here Dorian?" I spun around in his arms, running my hands over his hard torso, feeling his muscles flexing with every move of his hips.

His brown eyes met mine, and that smirk of his appeared. I wanted to kiss that smirk right off his face.

"I was having a chat with a friend of mine, and spotted you dancing like a teenager in her bedroom. So, I thought I'd get a better look." He was provoking me, as usual.

I leaned in close, rubbing my breasts against his chest, moving down his body then back up. He was completely in control of himself when my eyes met with his gaze. I thought I would have at least gotten a hiss out of him or some reaction. Oh well.

"What are you doing, Esme?" His calm voice had a bit more bite in it.

I swayed, enjoying myself whether he was dancing with me or not.

"I'm on Operation Get Esme Laid," I sang out in my drunk-ass voice.

That brought a reaction out of him. His eyes darkened, and his fingers gripped my waist a bit harder. I wished I knew what he was thinking, so of course drunk me asked. His head leaned in, his breath tickling my ear since my long hair had been braided to the side so my back could be seen.

"I'm thinking about fucking you and getting my curiosity out of my system." His words were low, and I felt the vibrations shiver down my skin, making me shudder.

I turned back around, pulling out of his grasp, my finger waggling at him.

"Too bad you wouldn't stoop low enough to fuck me in the on-call room, huh, Dorian? I would have rocked your world, but instead you couldn't pull that stick out of your ass, and you lost this bomb-ass pussy," I said, stalking away, feeling like a goddess for setting him straight. Even if I would totally regret it once I was sober and working with him the next day.

Lilith pulled me in for a hug and then held my hands, moving me with her to the beat.

"Your emotions feel strange, like a big weight was lifted off your shoulders but also some kind of regret. You okay?" Rose shouted as she danced next to me.

"Yeah, I just finally told my dick of a chief physician, who said he wanted to fuck me, that he missed his chance, and I had bomb-ass pussy," I responded. Rose stopped dancing. In fact, all three of them did. Echo immediately scanned the club, as if there was a threat.

"It's all good, guys. I've been dying to say that for a long time. I feel so free!" I tried to get Lilith to dance with me again, but she was apparently done.

"Come on, guys! Dance with me!" I pouted as I continued to shimmy and bob to the beat.

"Dorian was just here?" Rose asked, and I nodded. That bastard ruined everything, including my night out with the girls, it seemed.

"Yeah, he's an ass. Please, can we go back to having fun?" I tried again, not ready to let go of my drunken night of freedom. They looked at each other, having a silent conversation, and began dancing again, but it wasn't the same.

We stayed for another hour before they dropped me off at my apartment and went back to their men. I bet they had awesome sex, while I slept alone and dreamed of dancing under the stars with a man with a stupid smirk.

Chapter Five

Esme

It was official.

The dam had been broken, and the Esme I'd always wished I would be was out in the open. I woke up feeling like complete crap, but one thing I didn't feel was regret. I didn't care that I'd grinded on Dorian or told him how he missed his chance. I lived hard last night, and I loved it. I wanted that feeling to never go away, so I drank a big glass of water, took some pain reliever to help with my hangover, then went back to bed and slept it off until I had to get ready for the third shift again.

I was pleasantly surprised to see Dr. Liam working tonight on my floor instead of Dorian. Hopefully he had the night off, and I could enjoy my night without him glaring or making snide comments about me.

Melissa Ann was working with me again, so we were joking around all night between patients, and the shift flew by. After I clocked out, I went down to the cafe for a breakfast sandwich, settling down with some coffee at a small table in the corner. The sound of a chair moving across the floor made me look up, and Dorian dropped down into the chair across from me with a cup of coffee in his hand.

I'd had a very peaceful night without seeing Dorian, and of course he just had to ruin it at the last minute. If I would have gone home instead of eating here, I probably would have avoided him. No matter, I was done letting him get to me, so I sipped my coffee and started eating my breakfast.

He didn't say anything, and neither did I. We just sort of glared at each other while eating. When I was done and ready to go home to do some laundry and sleep, he rose with me and we walked our separate ways. It was an odd encounter, and I wasn't sure what to make of it.

I went about the rest of my day trying not to think about it at all. I'd been mostly successful until I fell asleep. I dreamed of his hands coasting over my skin and wanting him to touch me hard, but he wouldn't. He was just content to tease me.

When I woke, I was so sexually charged that I should have taken care of it myself, but I forgot to set the alarm and had to rush out the door.

One more day, then I would be off for two. I didn't have any plans, but Lilith had offered to help teach me some defense moves. So, I would see if she was up for it. Couldn't hurt to learn how to defend myself, just in case.

As soon as I walked into the ER, a fight broke out between two men who already looked banged up. Security had been standing there with them, so they were able to break them up quickly. Dr. Liam was there, checking them over with Melissa Ann, who had taken some steps back to protect her baby bump from the rambunctious men.

I looked over the paperwork from the nurse before and saw I had a few minutes to spare before needing to make my rounds.

When Melissa Ann and the doctor came over to the nurses' station, she started shaking her head.

"What's that all about?" I asked, and Liam, with his blue eyes and wavy hair, was the one to answer.

"Two men...one is dating the other's sister, and the brother accused the boyfriend of using his powers to seduce her. Then they got in a fight. One kid has the power to read minds." Liam looked over his charts and scribbled down some notes. This was not going to be a good day, if this was the first event of my shift.

"Are they okay?" I asked, and he nodded.

"Some cuts here and there, but that's it. No broken bones as far as we can tell. Might take the brother in for an X-ray to double-check his wrist. I'll tell you, things are starting to heat up again. This is the third set of patients in the past twenty-four hours dealing with someone with powers." He gave me a sad smile, and I knew how he felt. As a person who wanted everyone to be happy, healthy, and safe, this was not going to be good, and we as health professionals could see it coming a mile away. The citizens of Seahill were going to destroy each other.

Melissa Ann was oddly quiet as she sat down in her chair.

Liam gave me another smile before leaving the desk, and I waited till he was out of earshot before asking if she was okay.

"I'll be all right; it's just hard thinking about what kind of world I'm bringing this new baby into." She sighed and started typing her notes on the computer. I could see the worry in her eyes, and I understood it.

I wished there was something I could say to make her feel better, but there was nothing right now. The future wasn't looking so bright, but I hoped for all of mankind that we could put aside our differences and be a unified world. A pipe dream, but I wished for it every chance I got.

A smile grew on my face when I saw Charles walking through the ER in the early morning hours, on his way to physical therapy. He stopped to chat, and I couldn't help but grin at his charming ways. He was nice, and now that he had full use of his legs, he had been working out more. The athletic build looked good on him.

His brown hair was a tad bit longer, and I knew some lucky lady was running her fingers through it frequently.

"Everything going okay?" he asked with a big smile on his face.

"Yep. Just saving lives as best as we can. You know." I winked, and he laughed. It felt good to have these people in my life, that knew all the parts of me and seemed to like me anyway.

"I hear ya. Next time you come to HQ, we need to hook you up with a communicator, and then you should hang out. We've been busy, but somehow, we still find that chance to all sit together. It's nice."

I would love that.

"Maybe during my next two days off."

He ran his hand through his hair, and I watched him do it. He was good-looking, and I could appreciate that.

There was an awkward silent moment, so I broke it by asking how his therapy was going.

He looked down at his legs and patted them nicely.

"Good. They have no clue how I got them back to where they are, but they've helped me so much. Today's my last appointment, actually," His face was completely lit up, and I leaned in for a hug to congratulate him. His body was warm, and those muscles wrapped around me securely. I missed being touched.

"Well, you better get to it!" I pulled back from my hug and gave him a parting smile.

"Thanks, I'm sure I'll see ya soon." He waved and then walked toward the therapy department.

It was moments like this that I was proud of my gift.

They may or may not remember that Rose and Draco had saved me one day at the hospital months prior. A man had been brought in to the hospital unconscious, but once he had woken up, he was a threat to my life. They stopped him from killing me, and I knew I owed them a debt, even if I didn't say it out loud.

When Charles and Leon were taken to the hospital, both on the brink of death, I healed them. I also healed Charles' spine so that he could use his legs again. None of the society knew, as far as I could tell, and I wanted to keep it that way. I didn't want recognition for doing what I could. Even if helping them may have taken a few years off my life, I was happy I did it, and would do it all over again.

Chapter Six

Dorian

"Grab this and try to bend it in half." I held up a piece of rebar to Ajax, a veteran who lost everything he had once he came home. He had volunteered to host unlimited strength.

The man worked out nonstop and was very large, with black, shaggy hair and a dark beard. One would say in the old days that he looked like a pirate.

His big hands gripped onto the metal, and his muscles flexed. Slowly but surely, the metal began to bend and then snapped in two.

Excellent.

I'd created my own version of the Hero Society, and soon I was going to unleash them. Those do-gooders were no match for these better versions. Not clones, but now I had the same powers they possessed in my army. The strength, the empath, the shifter. I even had a computer geek, and a killer of my own. The only one I was missing was the magic, and I had little use for that. Magic was no match for the power of the gods.

Phillip's powers came from my father, Apollo, and I was privy to the same power, along with some handy others. But it wasn't constantly on like his was—mine was more like a TV that I could turn on when I wanted, checking the futures and following my own path that led where I wanted. His sights were set on the future where people like them were the heroes. They would be safe and live out their lives saving humans and protecting them. A happy ending.

I wanted to set them all free. No more hiding, no more fear. We were powerful and shouldn't belittle the gifts that were given.

"Keep practicing, making sure you gain control over these new powers," I said and moved to check the others' progressions.

Everything was moving along smoothly, and I had begun to realize that letting Emanuel fall to the heroes had been a positive development. He was wasting time, when all we needed was some blood from Draco. Years wasted.

But now, things were as they should be.

I checked into the future for a moment to see that no one would be in my office at the hospital as I flashed in.

The hospital was getting busier from the hate brewing outside, a perfect time for me to persuade others to join my side and be free.

I looked over the patients that had come in, and saw two had been documented as having powers, but only one had been checked in.

Without wasting time, I left my office and walked to the boy's room.

"Ron Presley." I grabbed the charts at the end of his bed and looked at the man in his twenties before me. He wasn't much to look at as far as build—definitely no fighter—but he was here because of a fight. He'd asked to be admitted for the night, and someone approved his stay. Odd.

He didn't say hello to me but stared at me with narrowed green eyes.

"I'm in," he said, and I tilted my head to the side, interested in what he was agreeing to.

"Care to elaborate?"

He looked out the window for a moment, lost in thought, before turning back to me.

"I'm tired of hiding and being hated because of my power. I'm not evil. I just wanna be me and not worry about being in a fight because of people being scared. So, I'm up for what you came down to ask."

This morning was interesting already.

"I read minds. I knew what you wanted when you came in. Figured I'd save you the breath."

The kid had spunk, I'd give him that. Mind reading was definitely a power I could use.

"When the time comes, I'll come to you," I said, and looked over his paperwork just in case.

"Is there a reason you decided to stay overnight? Your wounds hardly need any attention." I was curious, not that I had an issue with it. Wasn't my money he was wasting, so I couldn't care less.

He shook his head.

"I didn't want to go back to reality yet. It sucks out there."

It sucked everywhere, no matter the reality. I saw his head nod in agreement to my thought. Just as I was about to say something, someone knocked on the door.

"Hey, Ron, I'm about to leave, and I just—" Esme stopped speaking as soon as she saw me in with Ron. Her teeth nibbled on her lip in a way that suggested she was nervous. As soon as she noticed my eyes on that lip she let it go and stood straighter. She looked more confident, like she had yesterday morning when we had silent breakfast together.

She moved her eyes from me to Ron and walked over.

"I just wanted to check on you. Do you need anything before I head out?" She ignored my presence and gave her full attention to the boy.

He shook his head and looked out the window again, obviously done talking.

"Okay. If you need anything, just let Luce know. She's the day-shift nurse. Dr. Liam said you're clear to stay resting for the remainder of the day." She leaned in and touched her hand to his shoulder.

"It's going to be all right." She spoke to him sweetly and then walked off without sparing me a glance.

His gaze turned to watch her leave.

"The world would be in better shape if more people were like her," he commented, and I wanted to scoff. Maybe this kid would be better suited for Draco's little club, if he thought Esme was the optimal person to be in life.

"I'll be in touch," I stated and began my walk out of the room too.

"She wants you but doesn't like that she wants you."

I turned my gaze back at him and smirked.

"I know."

The feeling was mutual.

Chapter Seven

Esme

"Here." Lilith handed Leon a bottle of vodka to help take the edge off.

He'd been stabbed in the shoulder, close to an area where there looked to be a bullet scar.

I finished stapling him up and bandaging the wound.

"I can't believe someone tried to stab you." I looked at Charles and then back at Leon to make sure he was all set. I handed him some pain reliever and told him to take as needed. I knew I wasn't technically allowed to prescribe anything, but this wasn't exactly a legal job, and he'd needed it.

He thanked me and went back to drinking to help with the pain, ignoring the pills.

Charles had been silent since they had arrived. I'd been hanging out with Rose, sipping tea while chatting about a book she'd been dying to read when Lilith and Charles stormed in with the bleeding Leon. We went to the medical room immediately and I got started on fixing him. Thankfully that one stab wound was it, and the man who attempted to hurt Charles—that Leon had jumped in front of—had been taken to the police station and charged with assault.

"Things are getting nasty out there," I commented, and Leon scoffed.

"People are acting out in fear; it's never good when they do that," Lilith commented and leaned in to rest her head on Leon's good shoulder. She was not all smiles now. She was concerned and scary serious.

"Is there anything that can be done?" I asked. It had been a question I'd been wondering lately, and I hadn't been able to come up with a solution. No matter what those with powers said or did, there would be those who wouldn't accept them. They'd fear them, even the good ones. It was times like this that made me nervous that people would lash out and become the monsters that they are being made out to be.

"I think it just has to run its course. We keep helping as best as we can," Leon answered and turned his head to kiss Lilith's forehead.

"War is coming, and it's not going to be pretty." Lilith sighed, and the whole room turned solemn.

War. It did seem imminent right now.

"I wonder if that person you guys have been looking for is behind all this madness—creating their army from the chaos." I voiced my thought aloud, and they all looked at the floor or the wall.

"No clue," Charles said, and then there was silence.

I wished the bad guy would just make his presence known, and then they could fight them, ending this whole thing. I had faith in these people. In the end, I know everything will be righted. Something or someone will bring them all together.

After that depressing conversation, we moved to the chill room and watched a movie. I shared a big blanket with Rose while Lilith snuggled Leon and Charles sat in the chair by himself. Halfway through the movie, AJ joined us and we just enjoyed relaxing for a change.

I spent my second day off cleaning my apartment and read two of the books Rose recommended. They were about the world of fae. I had been so consumed by the story of love and sacrifice I'd gotten the audiobook so I could listen to the hunter with the artist's soul and the high lords that loved her while I cleaned.

It may be fantasy, but the love between the two characters was the type of love I'd always dreamed of. They both would sacrifice their very lives so the other could be happy. They loved strong and would do anything for each other. They cherished each other and had accepted every strength and flaw equally. Embracing both.

The next day I was working the second shift, so I tried to sleep during the night but sort of failed.

I walked into work with a smile on my face even though I'd only slept for five hours.

Melissa Ann was off today so that was a bummer, but it happened, and I was friendly with the other nurses and doctors, so it was still going to be a nice day. Today I was helping out in the maternity ward. While I loved being around all the pregnant ladies and babies, it made my heart hurt sometimes. I always thought I'd have kids, but the reality that I might not live long enough to see them grow up made me too scared to have them.

Still, I helped deliver two babies, and was there for the three women who were in the postpartum care rooms with their newborns. It was sweet watching the new parents fawn over their bundle of joy while trying not to freak out over every squeak and snort. I'd had to go into their room more than once to ease their worry.

I was sitting at the nurse's station, doing the never-ending paperwork and thinking that I needed to get out more. I wanted to start dating again. I had kissed a lot of frogs, but if I wanted to find a prince, I'd probably have to kiss some more.

"Daydreaming at work. How very Esme of you."

"Speaking of frogs," I mumbled and tipped my face toward Dorian. I'd passed him once in the halls earlier—he'd been called in to do a complicated delivery. He'd been in that operation room for hours, as far as I knew, but the woman and baby were okay, so that was all that mattered now.

"Frogs?" He raised his eyebrows, and I looked over his appearance. His hair was messier than usual, and his five-o'clock shadow looked more like a seven o'clock one. But his eyes were stuck on me, waiting for me to answer his question.

"I'm tired of kissing frogs while looking for a prince. You are not my prince, so you are definitely a frog in this story," I said, still feeling that bravado inside me that I'd had days before. I was a changed woman, and there was no going back. He didn't laugh or make fun of my words to him; he simply held my stare before leaning in.

"I'm definitely not the prince in this story and never will be the good guy, especially where you are concerned." His low timbre made shivers dance across my skin. I heard him loud and clear, and I completely agreed with him, but the way his eyes were boring into me made my stomach flutter.

Not tonight, stomach, this man was the devil, and there was no way in hell.

We stared at each other for another moment before he smiled and rapped his knuckles on the desk, walking away without another word. I hated these weird encounters I kept having with him. There had been a change between us, and I wasn't liking it. He was paying me more attention than he had before, and while I was not giving into the attraction, it was still there no matter how hard I fought it.

The more I thought about Dorian, the more firmly I decided that I was going to go out tonight after shift to dance and get laid. I needed to get my mind off him once and for all.

My resolve gave me more pep in my step at the end of my shift, as I went into the quiet breakroom to grab my coat and wallet from my locker. I didn't care who the lucky guy was. Tomorrow I would start looking for something more real. Tonight was all about satisfying myself sexually so this flutter in my stomach would vanish whenever Dorian came near and stared at me.

I turned around to head out when I froze. Dorian was there and the look on his face was completely predatory.

"Have a good night, Dorian," I murmured before walking toward the door he was standing just in front of. He didn't say anything, but as soon as I was within arm's reach, his hand shot out and gripped my wrist, keeping me from going further.

"You're not going to fuck another man, Esme. If any cock is going to be inside you, it'll be mine."

Those words.

They shouldn't make my heart beat faster, but they did.

"You have no say in that matter," I said breathlessly, wishing I'd waited a few seconds to speak so I wouldn't sound so affected by his words.

His body moved and mine turned instinctively with his, facing each other. Every bell in my head was going off, warning me to back away.

"I do."

He took another step forward and looked down at my lips.

"Dorian." His name was part plea and part prayer. My mind didn't want him to do what he was leaning down to do, but my body was moving toward his, ready to feel what he'd give me.

We were inches away from each other's lips when I looked into his eyes.

"I hate you," I whispered before his lips descended on mine.

Chapter Eight

Esme

I was grumpier than ever the next day at work, so much so that Melissa Ann felt the need to corner me in the bathroom and make me talk.

"Girl. I'm done being around your pissy self. I'm the pregnant hormonal woman; you need to relax yourself before I get all riled up with you," she huffed, checking the stalls to be sure there was no one else in the bathroom.

"Dorian kissed me yesterday." I wasn't ever good at keeping secrets, and I wanted someone to talk to about it. While I knew she'd get all excited, she also knew Dorian was an asshole, particularly to me.

She bit her lips to contain her excitement and waited for me to continue before freaking out.

"He kissed me soft, and then hard, and dammit, I liked it. But that's not the best part! The best part would be when he got paged and left me standing there without another word." I was so frustrated. He knew what he was doing. Somehow, he guessed I was going out to get laid last night and wanted me thinking about him so I wouldn't do it. And he succeeded.

Melissa Ann looked at me with a face that said I was a dumbass.

"You do know he's the chief physician in the hospital, right? He's a busy man. It's not like he made his own pager go off."

A point I was well aware of, but still. I was frustrated, both sexually and mentally. I didn't want to waste brain space thinking about the man who'd been a complete asshole to me.

He would be the type of guy to screw you then kick you out of his house. I didn't want that! I wanted a man to screw me senseless then cuddle me afterwards. Dorian was no cuddler. Nothing about him screamed gentle at all. His kiss last night was gentle for all of two seconds before the heat took over us and the devouring began just like before.

"I hate him," I told her, and she nodded.

"Fine line between love and hate, my dear."

I shook my head at that statement. There was no love between us, that was for sure. Now lust, I could agree on. That was there in spades, but love? No way in hell could I fall for a man like him, and I doubted he was even capable of love. I doubted he loved anyone but himself.

"You know my vote, but I can see you are going to fight just letting the man have his way and getting it out of your systems, so what are you thinking?" She knew me well, but the fact is I had no idea what I was going to do. That was what was frustrating me—despite everything, my heart kept speeding up whenever I saw him today, even in passing. I didn't want it to.

"I don't know. He isn't the man for me." I leaned against the wall and sighed.

"He doesn't need to be the man for you, but there has always been a pull between you two. You're both losing the fight of denying it. My vote is give in and see where it goes. He plays asshole hard, but I bet he'll love even harder once he realizes it."

I wasn't holding out for love with Dorian. That was hopeless, but maybe it was time I let my body lead with him. It was obvious that was all he wanted. Maybe after that we could move on. He'd go back to ignoring me, and I could find love without this sexual tension getting in the way of everything.

"Thanks for waking me up, Mel." I walked over and gave her a hug. She always knew when I needed a smack on the head, and this was what she did. I felt officially smacked on the head.

"Just name the firstborn after me, and we'll be even," she joked, and I pulled back to laugh.

"Evil woman."

We left the bathroom, and I indeed felt lighter.

I was in uncharted waters, but I knew where the lighthouse was, and he was currently staring at me with hungry eyes.

Feeling brave after my talk with Melissa Ann, I walked over to him and stood close. If I didn't get this out now, I might never feel like it was the right choice.

"You win," I whispered, while looking around making sure no one heard me. When his eyes met with mine again, they were furrowed in confusion. Did he not get what I was saying?

"And what is it I won, exactly?"

An exasperated sigh escaped my lips. Did I really have to spell it out for him? I thought we were on the same page here.

"You win my body, but never my heart. Just so we're clear." I was laying that out there right now. My heart was going to have very thick walls and a moat surrounding it when I was around him.

"I never wanted your heart, Esme."

I didn't flinch at his words because at least we were both in agreement that this was completely for release and not love.

He didn't say anything else, and I kinda thought he was going to drag me off somewhere to take advantage of my mood right now, but he didn't. He just stood there looking at me, an unreadable expression on his face.

Right. We were back to these awkward silent moments that had been happening frequently between us lately.

"So, I'm going to get back to work. I'll, uh, page you." I turned and walked off.

I'll page you. Wow.

No wonder I was still single.

Work went by quickly and then the next day Dorian was off. I thought we would have jumped each other already, but he didn't seem like he was in a rush, and that sort of bothered me. Had I been the only one that was feeling this undeniable physical attraction between us? Maybe he only wanted me because I was denying him, and now the challenge was over.

Chapter Nine

Dorian

It was chemical attraction, plain and simple.

I needed to fuck Esme until there was nothing left but heavy breaths and fast-beating hearts between us.

It had been two days since I checked into the future and saw her with someone else, another man touching her creamy skin and kissing her, feeding from that hunger she had brewing inside her.

I moved without thinking toward the breakroom and made her think of nothing else but my touch. If she needed relief, then I would be the one fucking it into her.

She thought she would just page me whenever her need arose, but I doubt she would be that brazen. Although she had walked up to me with a determined look on her face when she claimed I'd won her body but not her heart.

I scoffed at the thought. Her heart was never on the table. Laughable that she was thinking she needed to put that out there. A few fucks and that would be it.

But for today, my desire for her had to be put on hold.

In order to stay immortal, I had to infuse the blood of the gifted with my own. It was a process that took a few hours, and I was bedridden until it was over.

I watched the infusion machine churn my gold-tinged blood with the donated blood of a god-powered man.

There were always people donating, not thinking about their powers when they did it. I used to take the donation from the people on the streets as I found them, but the hospital had so much now that I hadn't needed to get my hands dirty for quite some time.

Two hours left.

My eyes closed, and I attempted to clear my head and rest, but that didn't happen.

Instead I thought of all the ways I was going to enjoy my prize.

By the time the machine beeped, signaling that my transfusion was done, I was rock hard and pissed off that she'd somehow made me want her as badly as I did.

I stood and took care of cleaning the machine before getting dressed in simple clothes—jeans, boots, button-up shirt, and a jacket.

Though I wouldn't be wearing them for long, it would at least keep the chill off my back. The weather had warmed slightly, so instead of snow falling, we had rain.

It might drop down into freezing temps by the morning, though. Seahill was a bitch in the weather department. No one knew what she would do.

Esme should be getting off her shift soon, and then she'd walk to that shitty apartment of hers that was nearby. I could bring her back to my apartment, but I was anticipating that some material items would become collateral damage from this heat between us. Better her things than mine.

I flashed into my office and quickly exited the room on foot in search of the woman who was responsible for my vexed mood.

She wasn't hard to find; I had seen where she was going to be from the future sight, but what

I hadn't seen was Dr. Liam smiling at her, romantic interest clear as day on his face.

Interesting. I wondered how long this has been in the making.

As if she could feel me walking toward her and the doctor, her eyes met mine, and her eyebrow arched as if to ask why the hell was I here.

"Let's go."

My words came out harsh, and Liam's spine straightened at the tone.

"Dorian. I didn't know you were here. You've gotta get out of the hospital, man, and enjoy your time off." He laughed, thinking I was here because I was a workaholic. Wrong.

I didn't acknowledge him, instead keeping my focus on Esme.

"I'm almost done, if you wanna wait." She spoke softly and then walked around Liam to the computer. His gaze was moving back and forth between us, and even though I knew he could tell something was different, it didn't stop him from stepping closer to her, blocking me from her view.

"I'll see you around, Esme. Let me know if you need a ride on Sunday. It's really not an imposition at all."

I was on edge already, and his offer just pushed me over into a territory that was not safe for humans. But I remained unaffected on the outside, smiling coolly while seething inside. I plan on fucking her so thoroughly tonight that she wouldn't spare him a thought, let alone ride in his car.

"Thanks, Liam." Her words were rushed, and not completely dismissive.

He took his leave, giving me a look that said he wasn't going to bow out.

Good thing I was the villain in this story. He could have her when I was done. I'd use her body and then when this need was gone, he could have what was left. Maybe she'd even offer up the doctor that heart of hers.

"I think you'd make an adorable couple." I still wore the mask of indifference on my face when she turned to look at me. She gazed at me for a minute then turned her eyes elsewhere, a muscle in her jaw flexing as if she was trying not to lay into me with her thoughts on my behavior. Perfect, the backbone she'd found was soft again.

"It's none of your business. Now, I'm assuming you're thinking you're going to call in whatever this is, but I'm tired and definitely not in the mood now. So, you can go back to wherever you slithered out from. Maybe tomorrow."

She left for the breakroom, and I stood there for a moment, considering my next move. I could let her have tonight and cause some chaos in Seahill with one of my creations. That would at least burn some of this energy out of me. Or I could follow her and assist her into being in the mood. Both easy tasks.

Chaos of the mind, my only solace from a hell created in paradise.

I'd favored that saying for a long time. When my mind was in chaos, I was able to feel something other than the pain of living this life of hell on earth.

Esme was my chaos, and right now I was burning for her.

She had already left the breakroom and was out the door when I caught up to her. Not even the pouring rain could put out the spark that would surely ignite with us together.

Chapter Ten

Esme

I felt him behind me, and I knew he was going to pull one of his favored "grab me by the arm and kiss me" moves.

So I decided to act first.

I spun around and waited for him to reach me. It took all of ten seconds, and our lips clashed in the downpour of rain.

He groaned into my mouth, and I was greedy for every sound he made.

I'd been frustrated and stupidly self-conscious that he didn't want me once I became available to him, but the way he was kissing me suggested otherwise. Dorian wanted me badly—very badly.

"You're not going with Liam anywhere," he growled while his fingers gripped my waist, pulling me tighter to his body.

"I'm not your pet, I can do what I want." I moaned as his mouth moved down my neck and back up to my lips.

Inches from connecting again, he spoke against my mouth.

"You're wrong." He pressed his lips hard to mine, punishing me for voicing my thoughts. My hands wrapped around his neck, snaking my fingers through his soaked hair while we ravished each other's mouths. Well, I was in the mood now. In fact, I was more than in the mood. I was on fire for him.

"My apartment," I mumbled, wanting to feel him against me immediately.

"I won't be gentle," he warned. I didn't care. I didn't know what kind of man Dorian would be in bed, but I knew he wouldn't be the sweet, make-love type of guy. I was expecting lots of hard fucking. Twist my arm a little, but I was okay with that. Did anyone ever turn down a hard fuck session? No. The answer was no.

"I never asked for gentle."

With those words out in the air between us, he pulled back and gestured for me to lead the way.

The short walk up to my apartment was agonizing. We kept our hands to ourselves, and I don't know why he didn't touch me, but I knew my reason was because I wouldn't stop for the rest of the night. I was done with this fight between us; I wanted to feel our bodies move together and let him use me.

I unlocked my apartment and turned around to face him.

"You better not be a bad lay." I don't know why I said it—maybe to feel stronger, like this was nothing to me besides sex. And it was just that, but somewhere deep in my stomach I felt that flutter.

"The worst." He smirked and reached out to push back some of the soaked hair that was plastered to my face. The touch was surprisingly soft, but I knew it wouldn't last.

We stood there for what seemed like forever before I moved into my apartment, and he followed, closing the door behind him.

With our gazes locked on each other, one by one we started taking off our wet clothes until both of us were bare. Only then did our stare roam over what was right in front of our eyes.

Oh my God.

God.

Dorian was a god.

There was nothing but hard muscle and smooth skin that covered every dip and bump.

Heat blossomed over my body, knowing that that man was going to be touching me.

"Get on the bed, Esme," he ordered, and my eyes flew up to his. The smirk that was on his face at the door was gone now. This man looked like he was barely holding on and might snap at any minute.

Feeling like a dangerous woman, I turned around and slowly crawled up the bed with my ass in the air, a perfect tease for his eyes.

I heard him growl, and I smiled. Yes, teasing him was quite amusing.

When I turned around, settling in nicely against the pillows, I waited to see what he was going to do with me. I was his prize, after all. He wanted to fuck the curiosity out of his system, so he would probably get right to it. I was ready.

Slowly, just as I had done, he reached the bed and moved toward me, his hands skimming my legs, moving up and splaying against my hips.

His lips went right for my nipple, making my back arch from the touch. He moved from one to the other, making sure neither breast was feeling lonely, before hot, open-mouth kisses with swirls of tongue moved up my chest and neck, then landed on my lips.

"Never thought a temptress lay beneath the sweet." His hand moved down my hip and gently touched my core. He rubbed little circles over my clit before plunging one finger inside me. I cried out, and he reveled in the taste of it against his lips.

As soon as he was moving his finger inside me, it was gone.

In a flash that hand was spreading my legs to accommodate his body between them. This was it. I was going to have sex with Dorian, the last person on earth I ever thought I'd be in this position with.

There were no words spared when he pushed into me slowly, the exact opposite of what I thought he'd do. He was unhurried, like he had all the time in the world to fuck me.

Our eyes both watched as he sank deep into me. No sight would ever top this.

Or at least I thought that, until his brown eyes moved back to mine. There were so many emotions in them, and I swear I'd never seen anything as beautiful as the look he was giving me right now.

As if sensing my thoughts, he pulled out and thrust back in hard.

I cried out from the sudden attack of pleasure, and that was it—the soft was done, and the hard took over. Dorian unleashed himself on me, my leg coming up to wrap around his pistoning hip, my hands on his arms, nails digging into them to the point of breaking skin.

My back arched, and my head tipped back in euphoria.

He pulled out and flipped me over with ease, keeping me smashed against the mattress as his body covered mine, hands intertwined in mine while he pushed back in, his hips smacking my ass with every thrust.

Our hands gripped the other so hard I thought our fingers might break, but as that feeling of release raced through me, I couldn't care if all my bones were breaking. This orgasm was going to shatter me anyways.

And it did.

I screamed into the mattress, and his pace hastened, drilling me over and over until his roar echoed around my apartment and his release overtook him as he buried his head into my neck.

There was no going back for us—our course had been set, and we were going under.

Chapter Eleven

Esme

The first time wasn't the only time. In fact, Dorian had to have some power running through his veins to have that sort of stamina.

I was exhausted in the best way and had fallen asleep across his sweaty torso after the last bout of fucking.

Being alone in the bed when I woke up was not a surprise, but it didn't stop my heart from dropping in my chest. Dorian screwed me until my legs were incapable of walking, and I had passed out with a sated smile on my face.

I rolled over onto my back and thought about the way Dorian possessed my body like it was made for him to play with.

There was no telling if he would want more, or if last night was enough for him, but at least I had the memories that would last until I died. He definitely set the bar high for any future lovers.

Getting out of bed was a bit challenging; my legs were fatigued, but I made it to my bathroom and grabbed my robe from the back of the door.

Coffee was a must right now.

I walked back out into my living room, heading for my small kitchen, and was shocked to stillness at the form leaning against my small table.

Instantly I schooled my expression to not show my surprise to see Dorian sitting there, half-naked and drinking coffee, after last night.

"I figured you'd be out the door as soon as I passed out," I commented as I made my way over to the pot and poured myself a cup.

"The thought did cross my mind, but the idea of a morning fuck before work won me over." He smirked, and my cheeks turned pink. This man was insatiable, and even though there was definitely a soreness between my thighs, my core was getting wetter by the second just seeing that face of his.

"So, I take it the curiosity is still there then?" I sat down across from him at the cafe table and took a sip of my drink. Good Lord, did he like his coffee strong. His brown hair was messy, but those eyes of his looked bright and revived. I liked that look on him. It was much better than the soulless-asshole expression he usually wore.

His lips frowned at my question though.

"It would appear to have intensified, actually."

Even though I didn't want to admit it, much like he hadn't either, I felt the same. Hopefully things would calm down shortly because I didn't want to imagine trying to work with him with this powerful attraction between us.

"If you're thinking what I'm thinking, then things are going to get interesting at work," he stated calmly, and I shook my head. What did I get myself into?

"I thought this was going to be a one-night thing; we can't let this need get in the way of our lives. If it starts to, then it's over."

He lifted his mug up in agreement, and I raised mine to clink it against his. It seemed like we were both on the same page for now: enjoy this for what it was, when we needed it, and let it be just that. No fuss.

"Well, I've got to do some errands around sooo…" I let the end of my sentence trail off. I was ready for him again, and I wanted it now. Having errands was just an excuse to suggest we get the fucking underway.

His eyes sparkled with amusement, and his lips widened, giving me a rare full-teeth smile that very few have had the pleasure of seeing. He really should do it more often, even though it went against his asshole persona.

"So," he said, and then the mugs were briskly set on the table, and he carried me back to bed where he made the morning count in all the right ways.

After we chased our releases together and became a heap of sweaty lovers in my comforter, he kissed me hard then got dressed. Before he left, he sat down on the bed where I lay wrapped in the blanket.

"Where are you going on Sunday?" He wasn't demanding my answer, just curiously asking.

I stretched my legs, feeling every little ache from my body being used in ways I'd never felt before.

"I'm going home to Magnolia to see my parents. Just a one-night trip, but with everything happening in Seahill, they are feeling antsy. So I'm easing their minds with a visit."

He watched me snuggle my bed like it was heaven, which it was right now.

"I'll take you," he offered, and I looked at him like he had grown another head.

"What?"

"Yes, the statement is difficult to understand. I'll take you to your parents for the day. Magnolia isn't but an hour and a half away." He reached over and pulled down the comforter to display my breasts. Weird. I didn't feel like covering myself back up; he'd seen me naked, and there was no reason to be shy now.

"You don't have to. I was going to rent a car and drive. It's not a big deal. Plus, you'd have to be around people, and we both know that's not your strong suit." I was making a valid point. Even though Dorian was a very good doctor, he didn't "people" well. He just fixed them, and that was it.

"I'm taking you."

He stood and left before I could form a protest.

I probably lay in bed for another hour just thinking over everything that had occurred in the past twelve hours. Liam had been flirting with me. Turns out we grew up in the same town. He was five years older than me, so we weren't in school together, but it was nice to talk about familiar places with someone who'd been there.

Then Dorian had strutted in and all but knocked Liam out of the way to get to me. It was awkward and sort of nice at the same time. I'd never been fought over before, although I doubt Dorian would put up much of a fight. He had me, and while things might continue sexually between us, if someone wanted to date me I doubted he would stand in the way.

I kept reminding myself that our night spent together wasn't a big deal, but something heavy was wrapping around me, and I prayed I had enough common sense to shrug it off.

Chapter Twelve

Esme

"Yes! Oh God, right there," I hissed into Dorian's ear, trying to keep my voice down as his hands gripped my ass tighter while his cock nailed me to the shower wall of a bathroom in an empty patient room.

I turned my head to face him, and our lips met hungrily, and that was all I needed. My release tore through me, and of course he groaned into my mouth at the same time I cried out into his.

"I'm so glad you answered your pager," I moaned, pulling away from his lips and letting my head fall back against the tile.

He chuckled and lifted me off him gently. I grabbed some toilet paper and cleaned myself up while he took care of himself.

Once we were both all set to go out into the hospital again, I looked at him, and he at me.

This was an awkward moment if I'd ever experienced one.

"Thanks for that. I'll, um, see you soon." I walked to the door with my cheeks flaming, hearing him chuckle behind me as I left the bathroom. Apparently, Dorian had released a needy monster inside me last night. I swear, all I had to do was think about the way his hands gripped mine as he fucked me hard and I was like a cat in heat.

This morning hadn't been enough. No, apparently I needed him two other times in the past five hours. He had been available both times, and I was getting nervous what would happen when I felt the desire pop up and he didn't answer. Would I combust?

Yeah, I was feeling dramatic. But apparently once you gave your body to the devil for a night, he possessed it even when he wasn't around.

"Okay, spill. I know what you and the doctor have been doing because he hasn't been frowning as much, and you look fuckintoxicated. And don't give me that face—I made it up, but you look it." Melissa Ann walked alongside me as we journeyed to the nurses' station.

"I think he's turned me into an addict; I can't stop thinking about him and sex," I admitted. She laughed then glared at anyone who gave her a funny face from her outburst.

"Well, at least I was right about him being good in bed."

"And the wall, and the table. Really, anywhere." I covered my mouth after the words were already out. This was embarrassing.

Melissa Ann laughed some more then pulled me in for a hug.

"You're doing what you always wanted—living hard and fucking even harder. Until it becomes too consuming, enjoy that cock, Esme." She kissed my cheek and then we went about our night, checking on patients and administering medicine. Living hard and fucking harder. She was right about that.

Dorian had given me a nod as he left after his shift. No kiss goodbye or anything, and that was what I needed from him—to remind me that it was still indeed just physical between us.

Once my shift was over, I was wired from running around at the hospital, so I walked the few blocks over to the Hero Society headquarters, curious if anyone was around.

A small smile grew on my lips as I thought about how a few short months ago I had virtually no one but Melissa Ann as my friend, and now I had her, a family within the society, and a man to screw when I needed. Things were changing, and I couldn't complain.

Until the building I was walking by exploded.

My body was thrown into the street. After a few moments to regain my senses, I started evaluating myself for injuries. Everything ached, and my ears were ringing. I was vaguely aware of a sharp pain in my arm, but otherwise I knew I was okay. I looked around to see if anyone else was hurt, but there wasn't anyone there but me.

Then a woman stepped out of the damaged building. Her body seemed to be absorbing the fire around her. She saw me there in the road and ambled over. I tried to crawl away, but was too stunned to get far. I had no way to fight this woman. My powers wouldn't be useful here, and I had no combat training.

She had long black hair and purple contacts in her eyes. She was wearing punk rocker gear, black top with fishnet sleeves, and purple ripped jeans with studded black boots, and she looked good in it—I'd give her that. She crouched in front of me and reached out to touch my hair.

"Poor little fly, caught in a web and doesn't know why." The woman had a thick Spanish accent, and I smacked her hand away from me.

"Feisty. You'd do well with us. I can feel the energy in your veins, little fly. You've got something inside that you hide." She was peering at me like a cat looking at her next snack.

"Why'd you blow up that building?" I asked, trying to waste time until help arrived. Hopefully. Hero Society headquarters wasn't far from here; surely someone would come.

The woman looked behind her, and I tried to get up and make a run for it, but she grabbed tight to my leg and turned her head back to me.

"The owner was an old friend of mine. He needed to learn a lesson. No means no." She smiled, and I felt a knot in my stomach.

"I'm sure you feel better now. You should go out and celebrate."

She laughed at my obvious brush-off, and then went to touch me again when a male voice broke into the scene.

"That's enough."

Draco was standing ten yards away, his arms crossed over his muscled chest. Next to him was Asher, who was chanting to himself, eyes on the burning building.

Suddenly the air cooled even more, and rain began to fall over the fire, slowly working to put it out.

The girl looked like she was going to laugh at them but then turned to me again.

"This group wants us to be controlled. We want to be free. If they talk to you about joining, don't. They won't be around much longer if they stand in our way." I think, in this woman's own way, she was trying to help me. She stood and gazed at Draco and Asher with narrowed eyes. She lifted her foot and stomped it on the ground. The earth rumbled, and a shockwave moved through the pavement. Draco braced himself and wasn't moved, but Asher was thrown back a few feet from her energy release.

The woman took off running before they could attack and in seconds was gone.

Draco got to me first, checking me over.

"I'm all right, other than a bruised arm I think." Draco lifted me under the arms to help me stand.

"Should probably get an X-ray to be sure." Draco looked concerned, and I gave him a soft smile. He was right, and it was nice to see the emotion on his face. Normally he was very stoic,

90

but I was lucky to see him smile every once in a while.

"I agree, better safe than sorry." Asher was all smiles, and it was contagious. I nodded, and together they walked me to the hospital while asking me about what happened. It was clear the girl with the power was on the other side and thought I should join them. But she was wrong— that side was selfish and didn't care who they hurt. They wanted freedom and power to do as they wished. That type of thinking never did the world good. We needed to work together and help mankind find peace.

...If peace could still exist.

Thankfully the hospital was just as slow as when I left, so I was seen quickly by Liam and another nurse named Joann. X-rays were taken, and I was just waiting for the results when Dorian walked in the room. Both Draco and Asher jumped from their seats, looking like they were ready to fight the doctor.

Chapter Thirteen

Dorian

Draco's rage made a smile appear on my face. It was only a matter of time before I encountered them after they discovered the truth. But I knew, as they did, that I was untouchable. I was one of the best doctors in the world, and as far as humanity knew, I was a model citizen. To kill me would be the end of their Hero Society, and they would never recover.

Asher, the wild card in the mix, was looking at me with anger as well. Which was fine, too. He would have had a fighting chance on my side, but alas, he fell for a hero woman, and with her came the society.

Ignoring their looks of hatred, I walked over to Esme, who was looking at both men with a curious expression.

It seemed my long-time suspicions were correct. She had no idea who I was, or that she was technically sleeping with the enemy. I'd wondered it ever since Echo pieced together the journal, but she'd never shown me any signs that she knew. Normal hatred from me being an ass to her was there, but nothing beyond that. For some reason, they were hiding my identity from her. I'd seen all the possibilities of her future, so which one was Phillip aiming for? Something to ponder over later.

"Gentlemen." I gave them a nod and focused my attention on Esme. She'd seen better days, but as far as I could tell, she was fine. A bit bruised up, but she would live.

"No broken bones, but you might want to take it easy for the next few days." I looked at her chart then set it down so I could reach over and touch her. Both men tensed, and I wanted to laugh. Overprotective apes.

"I thought you went home?" she asked softly.

I did go home, but when I heard that she was hurt, I came in to see for myself. Liam and the others were child doctors, as far as I was concerned. If I was going to keep using her body like I had, then I needed her fit and healed. Too bad she couldn't use that power of hers to heal herself.

"You know no one is better than me. So here I am." She rolled her eyes, and I heard one of the men scoff.

Feeling every bit the antagonist I was, I reached over and ran my fingers down the side of her dirty cheek.

"I'm glad you're okay." That was a true statement.

When Monica came back to the mansion and told me what happened, and what the girl she'd seen looked like, I knew it was Esme. I flashed in quick and took the X-rays right from Liam's hands. I didn't trust him with her, so here I was, making sure Monica hadn't done anything permanent.

Her cheeks flushed, and her eyes lit up with surprise.

"Uh, thanks."

I wished I knew what she was thinking, but that wasn't a gift I was born with.

Feeling the stares of the two men around us, I removed my hand from her cheek and took a step back.

"Ice, rest, and maybe a shot of vodka for when you come out of the shock of being near an explosion. If you need anything..." I gave her a smirk before continuing.

"Just page me."

Without another word, or a chuckle at the pink on her cheeks turning darker, I left the room.

Draco followed me out while Asher stayed in the room with Esme.

When we were a good distance from the room she was in, I stopped and turned to face him.

"Can I help you with something?"

I lived for moments like this, and truly, it was everything I had wanted and more.

"Whatever you've got planned, end it. No more people have to get hurt for whatever shit you've been pulling." His voice was low, and while he looked angry as hell, his body showed nothing but control. He was always in control, never letting go except around his Rose.

"We're both trying to make the world a better place. You have your vision for what that is, and I have mine." We were the same height and body size. He worked out far more than I did, so while he looked like a lumberjack, I was more ninja-like, slipping under the radar of most.

His face morphed into a mask of nothing. He wasn't going to give me the satisfaction of seeing his riled-up emotions anymore.

"We will stop you. I'll not let mankind down again," he vowed, and I wanted to laugh. He'd been failing in his mission since he started. Although I had a hand in that, he hadn't ever succeeded in what he was created to do.

"I wish you luck." I turned to leave, but he stopped my movements with his next words.

"Leave Esme alone before you break more than her body. She doesn't deserve to be with a man like you. She deserves better."

He walked back to the room and closed the door behind him.

Draco didn't know who I was, or anything else about me.

Shrugging off his last words, I handed Esme's chart to the nurse who would document everything in the computer.

Liam was standing by my office door when I approached. His head lifted, and his arms were across his chest. His eyes were narrowed, and his posture was completely on offense.

"You need to leave Esme alone. She's too good for you. You're going to end up hurting her."

What was it with other men telling me what to do with a woman? It was starting to piss me off.

Esme was good, and I was bad. We were fucking, not getting married.

I didn't need to defend myself and my choices—I was over two thousand years old.

Instead of replying, I grabbed the handle of my office door and pushed through the entrance. As I walked past Liam, he put a hand on my shoulder, stopping me from advancing.

I didn't spare him a glance but calmly spoke.

"Remove your hand, or you will lose it."

His hand was gone, but he wasn't done with me, it seemed.

"You don't see it, but that girl is capable of giving an indescribable love to the man she chooses. Don't let her waste that love on you, a man who doesn't care about anyone other than himself and his high-profile career." He waited for me to say something back, to defend myself or to tell him to fuck off. But I wouldn't. I simply walked into my office and slammed the door in his face.

There was no fucking love between Esme and me.

It was lust, plain and simple. I wasn't capable of feeling that emotion anymore. Not since the days of the gods did I ever even know what love felt like. That was a long time ago, and that particular feeling had stayed in the past, where it belonged.

Chapter Fourteen

Esme

Draco and Asher had walked me home after my hospital visit. Asher gave me a hug goodbye, and I made Draco give me one. He wasn't really a hugger, but I had to thank them for helping me today.

As soon as they left, I went straight for the shower.

My body had an intense, all-over ache, and I was really dirty. I stayed in the shower for a half hour, and then stepped out to dry.

My arm wasn't too happy lifting above my head, so I slid one of my knee-length nightgowns up from my feet pretty easily without much pain.

I was tired, the events from today were finally catching up with me. But as I snuggled into my bed, Dorian's scent hit me, and I can admit I burrowed my nose in further to relish the smell.

It was clear as day that Asher and Draco were not fans of Dorian, but they had dealt with him on few occasions, as far as I knew. He probably pissed them off at some point. It wasn't hard to imagine.

He came back to the hospital to check on me. I was trying not to read into that, but it was difficult.

Maybe he just wanted to check on his fuck buddy. Can't have sex if I had to be hospitalized from an explosion. That was it.

My mind had settled with that explanation, but then my heart did a little flip as I fell asleep, remembering the warmth on my cheek when he touched my face and said he was glad I was okay.

The next morning, my body didn't feel any better. In fact, it felt worse. I guessed being thrown a few feet to the ground from an explosion would make you feel like shit. I rolled out of bed to take care of myself in the bathroom and swallow some anti-inflammatory pills to help with the ache.

I called Melissa Ann to see if she could cover my shift tonight, and she said she'd be happy to, needing the extra money to help pay for baby stuff. So, I grabbed myself some fruit from the kitchen and went back to my bed, lugging my laptop along for entertainment.

My face scrunched up in surprise when a knock on my door came at dinnertime. I left my bed, where I had stayed almost all day, to take a look through my little peephole.

Dorian was standing there, with bags in his hands.

I opened the door and gave him my best attempt at a smirk.

"You're a delivery boy, too? Is being a doctor not exciting enough for you?" I teased. Whatever he had in those plastic bags and to-go boxes would be welcomed. I had been thinking about what I wanted for dinner when he knocked.

"I like to live on the edge," he commented and set the bags down on the table then turned to me. In a matter of seconds, his hands were wrapped around my waist and his lips connecting with mine.

It didn't take long for that urgent start of a kiss to turn into a need for more. His hands roamed up my body, feeling me as if he had missed touching me.

I winced when his hand passed over my arm.

He pulled back instantly.

Shoot.

"You should ice it." He took a step back and let his hands drop from my skin.

"I did about twenty minutes ago."

He wasn't the only one with a medical background in the apartment.

"I'm surprised to see you here. Just getting off?" He looked like he had a long day at work, but then again, he sometimes pulled two shifts, working like a maniac. His hair was messy, and his top button was undone.

"I was hungry. There was a buy-one-get-one special." He started unpacking the bags. I was surprised he cared to use that free meal on me. A small part of my wall I'd erected started to shake.

"Don't look at me like that. I didn't buy you a puppy—it's food. Simple. You eat, then we fuck. I'm not your date." And the shaking wall stopped.

"Bad day?" I sat down at the table and looked at what he got. Sushi? It was buy-one-get-one from the expensive-ass sushi place a block over from here? Methinks Dorian has strayed from the truth in his story. I loved that place, and if they ever had buy-one-get-one on sushi, I would be as big as a sumo wrestler.

He sat down and let out an exhausted sigh that I wasn't sure I was truly meant to hear. He sounded tired.

"I've got a lot going on. Big plans and all." He picked up his chopsticks and started eating. I guess that was all he was going to say about that.

The first bite was heaven, and we spent the rest of our time eating in silence. It wasn't as awkward as some of the other encounters we've had, which was nice. I just kept thinking about what was happening here. Why was my stomach fluttering when I looked at him? Why did he bring me expensive but delicious food?

But I didn't know what to say.

"If you planned us eating and then fucking, we should have done the fucking first. I am so blissfully full." I sat back in my chair, completely sated. No way would I be shaken up like a soda bottle with all this food in my stomach.

His eyes narrowed and he was silent for a moment, maybe choosing his words before blurting them out.

"That was poor planning on my part."

I looked at the time, and saw it was a few minutes past seven. Only thing I was thinking about was reading until I went to sleep. Should I make him leave or wait till I don't feel so full? This whole situation felt strange, and I didn't know how to act.

Screw these thoughts. If I wanted something, I was going to take it. Live hard, right? Well, I'd finally been doing that, so I needed to keep it going instead of reverting back to that woman who just worked and did nothing else. I had to make the most of my life, for me and for my brother.

"I'm going to go lie on the couch and watch a movie. You're welcome to join me, and maybe I'll be up for screwing you later, or you can head out. Won't upset me either way." I stood and threw my trays in the trash.

After grabbing myself a glass of water, I walked over to my green couch, setting the cup on the end table beside it.

I went about flipping through my DVR, looking for a movie I'd wanted to watch but never had the time. Dorian was sitting at the table still, apparently trying to come to a decision about his evening plans.

There were a few choices: an action flick, a romantic comedy, and an emo romance.

Truthfully, the emotional one has been on the top of my list, but I doubted Dorian would want to watch that.

Meh, fuck him.

Emotional romance it was.

Dorian stood and threw his trash away and walked over.

Was he going to stay?

That stupid flutter in my stomach made my lips start to turn up, but then I stopped myself when I saw his face.

Chapter Fifteen

Dorian

I was honestly going to leave; I had too much shit to do.

But the look on her face had me sitting down, wanting to touch those lips that smiled at the thought of me staying.

If I stayed, I would get to be inside her body again.

It was probably twenty minutes that I debated leaving. Being here in the moment quieted all the buzzing thoughts in my head. She'd been a balm to me before, and right now I was good with that.

The movie was boring, and I'd never seen it before. A troubled teen and a young woman of faith who was dying of cancer. She changed him, and they fell in love. Then she died.

Unrealistic.

I'd seen men change for women, sure. But the unrealistic part was the love between them. Once love died, there was nothing left but pain.

Esme started to stir, breaking up my thoughts from going down that dark section of memory lane.

She snuggled into the couch pillow she rested upon and continued to sleep peacefully. She really didn't know who was in the room with her. The villain.

I stood to leave. She was no use to me asleep.

One last glance at her, and my doctor training kicked in. She was sleeping on her injured arm. If she continued to sleep like that, she would be in all sorts of pain when she woke up, possibly even getting thoracic outlet syndrome. I ran my hands down my face. I should leave her alone. She was taking up too much of my time even when I wasn't around her.

But, I couldn't leave her like that. The doctor in me refused.

Without waking her, I scooped her body up and walked her into her bedroom. As I was laying her down, those slender arms wrapped around my neck and pulled me down with her, her lips instantly connecting with mine.

I was surprised for a few seconds before giving in to her kiss and taking over.

There was no rushing, just feeling, which turned to a hungry devouring.

That slip of a nightgown she wore was gone, as were my clothes. I needed to feel her creamy skin against mine and slide inside her waiting core.

We didn't speak, all just dancing tongues and hot kisses while our bodies connected, finding our release in each other.

Once we were done, she kissed me again, went to clean up herself, then crawled back into bed.

"You can go now if you want," she mumbled against her pillow, and was out again.

I chuckled to myself. I thought I was going to be using her for her body, but tonight she turned the tables on me, using my body for her own pleasure.

Staying the night was tempting, but I had been needing to leave for two hours.

I got dressed and walked out her door, flashing back to the mansion as soon as her door closed behind me.

"Good, you're back. I'm tired of waiting. This city is in chaos, now is the time to take control," Ajax grunted while sitting on the couch. Monica was sitting on the other end.

The others were in their own rooms. They were quite the group of misfits.

"You're not ready, but soon."

"The fuck we aren't."

The small smile that had been on my face from Esme's stunt was gone, and now I was annoyed. Before he could even blink, I was in front of him, hands around his neck, and then I flashed him to the wall. My grip was the only thing keeping his body up against the wall. He tried to pull my hand off his neck but like I had said before, he wasn't ready. He needed to become one with his borrowed powers. Until then, we would wait. Seahill was going to destroy itself no matter what. Draco and his crew were powerless to stop that.

I pulled my fingers off of his neck, and he fell to the floor with a loud thunk.

"I've been alive since the days of the gods. You're ready when I fucking say you are. You want the future I've promised? Then you follow my lead. Until then, learn to control your powers."

He looked at me and nodded. I understood his impatience, but we had time.

Nothing was going to change the future I'd set into motion. I'd seen it, and so far everything had passed that led to my chosen outcome.

I walked out of the room without another word. All the energy I'd expended with Esme was back, and I was restless.

My room in this compound was simple. I preferred to keep it that way. A rolled bed on the floor, and the rest was for training. Nothing was personal here. I knew the others wouldn't double-cross me, but I didn't want anything that could be used against me in any way.

I stripped out of my clothes, standing in the middle of the room in just my boxers. Calming my mind, focusing on every beat in my chest, expanding with every sound in the room, then the rest of the house.

At first, I moved slow, flexing every muscle, feeling the air beneath my fingers.

Over the centuries, I'd attempted to calm my taste for revenge with the masters of Asia, learning the Shaolin Kung Fu from the monks themselves, among other martial arts. Patience was the key to all of them.

For hours, I moved across my training floor, fighting invisible men. I grabbed my sword from the wall and worked on my form.

I was sweaty, and my muscles were aching from the training, but I finally felt like I could let my mind rest when I fell asleep.

Shifting my weight back, I raised my sword over my head and threw it like a javelin at the punching bag in the corner. It hit the bag dead center, and I smiled. My aim had always been a gift. I never missed.

I showered in the bathroom attached to the room and then passed out on the bedroll.

Chapter Sixteen

Esme

"Are you going to use that extra syrup?" Mina asked, and I shook my head. AJ's sister was adorable but feisty.

Everyone at the Hero Society was sitting in the kitchen area, eating a glorious breakfast that Janie had made. Echo had saved Janie when she was kidnapped because of her power to instantly remember things that she'd seen. It turned out okay, but she hadn't wanted to go home. Instead she made herself comfy in one of the apartments above the restaurant and started using all that knowledge to try new hobbies. Cooking was the one she enjoyed the most, so she would cook everyone meals when we were around.

This morning happened to be such a day.

The crew was looking tired and slightly run-down.

I knew the feeling.

It was hard living in a city where everyone hated you. I wasn't out about my powers, but I still felt their pain. This group was quickly growing from friends to family, and they'd welcomed me in with big, open arms.

Mina was chowing down on her extra sugary waffle, I had French toast and some eggs, and others were digging into their own delicious breakfasts that Janie had made to order.

"I don't know how you always eat that much and stay so thin. Maybe you do have powers after all," Leon commented, and Mina stuck out her tongue at him in a sisterly way.

"So, is anyone else going to address the elephant in the room?" Rose asked, and my fork paused midway to my mouth. Did I do something wrong?

"I don't know what you're talking about." Phillip grinned, and everyone else was looking in different directions like they weren't ready to talk about what Rose was bringing up. Okay, this was weird.

"Uh-huh. So, there isn't anything you want to...ya know, get out in the open?" She was egging him on, so at least now I knew it wasn't about me.

"I'm boning your brother."

All heads turned to Mina, who was sitting next to me in a long-sleeved purple shirt with a hoodie that had cat ears on the top of her head.

She continued eating like what she just said wasn't a big deal.

"I knew it! My girl is tapping that!" Lilith clapped and smiled, clearly excited. Everyone else laughed, including Draco.

Rose shoulder-bumped her brother, and he just smiled at her sweetly, making my chest hurt a little. Being around Phillip and Rose reminded me so much of my brother, Eli. They had such a close relationship that one would think they shared that twin connection, like Eli and I had.

All but Draco and AJ—who I'm pretty sure was trying to block out this whole conversation—were congratulating the couple and busting their balls about trying to keep it a secret. Obviously, Phillip was okay with this all happening because he was the only one who had the means to know it was coming and do something differently.

Mina, being a woman who didn't hold anything back, told us that Phillip had set it up to be this way all along. He found AJ, but knew AJ needed the time to grow into his own, and Mina to look for him. Mina was Phillip's soul mate. He knew that by helping AJ, he'd also help the woman he was destined for. She was pissed at him in the beginning because he could have reunited them sooner but came around quickly. It's hard to hold back when someone knows you are their future and will do anything for you.

Phillip must straddle the right path to make sure the best possible future happens for us. It must have been hard for him to stay away and not rush to the girl of his dreams as soon as he knew. He'd been in pain too, by staying away.

It was the type of love I'd always wanted, and while the two were completely different people, I could see how it would work. She was the queen to his king of the city. She would keep him on his toes, even with him being able to see the future.

"How's the arm feeling?" Draco asked, and I smiled. He was kind and caring through that tough-looking mask he wore. Watching those he cared about die had taken a toll on him, but I could see he was really trying to let everyone in.

"It's all right, just sore. I will survive."

I moved my arm, testing the range of motion. It was fine. I was lucky I hadn't been closer to the explosion.

He nodded.

115

"Before I forget, I'm heading to Magnolia to see my parents tomorrow, so no one get hurt for twenty-four hours, okay?" I looked them all in the eye, giving them my best nurse stare and a few of them laughed. I guess the look wasn't as badass as I was trying to make it.

"I don't foresee any trouble. We should manage a day without needing your services." Phillip wasn't smiling as he said those words. Was there something else he saw that he wasn't saying aloud?

"Good."

Everyone finished eating their food, then Leon and Lilith went up to their room with claims they wanted a nap. Everyone knew better. Rose and Draco settled themselves in the chill room on their chair while she read a book and Draco just enjoyed her company.

Phillip and Mina got into a very interesting conversation about how to stop pollution in the ocean. Mina was going to whip that boy into a weapon for her own use, I could tell. Thankfully she was on the side of good and would make him do things like end world hunger or save all the kittens.

Echo and Asher headed off to go hike in the snow. They were outdoorsy, and while I wasn't much of a nature girl, I could appreciate the beauty of simply being one with the woods.

So then it was just AJ, Charles, and me. Charles left for the training facility below, intent on using his new strength as much as he could.

"Wanna come play in the command center with me?" AJ asked awkwardly, and I grinned.

"Of course."

AJ was a nice boy. Really smart, but what I think I loved about him most was his ability to not let the world get him down. Even when things were going wrong left and right, he stayed positive.

"I control what I can and let go of what I can't. I learned that a long time ago," he said, and then we became the eyes of the city for a while, watching over Seahill like a protective mother waiting to step in when needed. Together.

Chapter Seventeen

Esme

I was sitting in an Aston Martin with Dorian.

I was totally sitting in an Aston Martin with Dorian, on our way to my parents' house.

"You really didn't have to drive me. I would have been fine," I said, and he just gave me a look and turned his eyes back to the road.

"Well, don't think this earns you anything special. You're not getting anal, or anything close, just for driving me." I shrugged and wiggled to get a bit more comfortable in the smooth seat.

Dorian looked at me for a hot minute, then his mouth opened, and he laughed. A full-on belly laugh, and I couldn't help but stare at him. In all the time I'd known Dorian, I'd never seen him look so...normal, with his dark jeans, black button-up shirt, and a smile on his face.

I was looking pretty cute, if I did say so myself, in an off-the-shoulder green sweater dress and tight leggings tucked into boots.

We had only been driving for thirty minutes, and I was already starting to regret agreeing to Dorian playing chauffeur.

"So, you're just going to drop me off and do whatever you do, right? I'll call you when I'm ready to go."

I stared out the window, enjoying the beautiful scenery, praying he would just agree, and that would be it.

"I'm not going somewhere else."

Dammit.

"I can't have you around my parents. They're going to think we're dating or something." I really hadn't thought this through. I should have just told him no or snuck out before he came to pick me up.

"They won't approve of a friend bringing you home and staying in the room with you?"

"Yeah, no." I shook my head. Oh God, my parents were going to freak.

"Plus, we aren't friends," I reminded him. We were having sex. And sometimes eating together.

He seemed to think on my words before speaking.

"Just tell them we're dating."

I froze.

Did I just hear him right?

"We aren't dating."

"I'm quite aware. We pretend, and at least this way I can make you scream and no one will blink an eye."

That was his reasoning? We lie to my parents, and then he can screw me, and they won't care?

"Is that all you care about? Making me scream? Not lying to my parents? Or pretending to be my boyfriend? I mean, seriously, have you ever even dated before? Do you know how to be in a relationship?"

Yeah, I was freaking out, but I had a right to be. This was one big and bad decision. My mom was pretty insightful, she would see through this. And my dad! He would be all protective of his daughter.

Sweat beads broke out on my forehead when I realized that Dorian was going to hear everything about me. About Eli. This was too personal. We were just supposed to be screwing. I would be vulnerable to him, and I didn't want that.

"My twin brother died when I was sixteen," I blurted out, grasping for information I could give him, so he was learning about me and my past from my own mouth instead of my parents. At least this way he would understand when the air in the room shifted to sadness—it was because we missed him so much. His death changed us all in many ways.

"How did he die?" Dorian asked calmly, and I started telling him everything. Well, everything except my gift. I wouldn't give him that tidbit, and I knew my parents didn't even know, so I was good there.

He listened quietly as I told him about Eli and about growing up in Magnolia, a small town with a very homey feel. I told him about my need to become a nurse to help people and control the things I could. Which still wasn't much, but I tried.

Once we pulled off the highway and made our way through the streets of my hometown, I started to feel all the memories tug me to follow them.

"Helping the sick and injured has always been second nature to me. It's the healthy and mobile that I don't care for." Dorian was trying to distract me, but I would bite. I knew nothing about him, and since I opened up about my life, I was hoping he would do the same for me.

That hope fell flat when he didn't say another word and we pulled into my parents' driveway.

They lived in a nice two-story home on an acre of land that had four bedrooms and three baths, surrounded by big trees. My favorite part of the house had always been the front porch. It wrapped all the way around and had a swing on the back.

Dorian parked the car and turned to face me.

"Relax, everything's going to be fine."

His hand nestled itself through my hair, pulling my head toward his as he leaned in.

The kiss was surprisingly sweet, and even comforting.

My body started to relax and focused on his lips against mine.

When he pulled back his eyes were locked on mine as they opened.

"Showtime," he whispered, then went about getting his jacket on and stepping out of the car. He walked around and opened the door for me, which was a tad over the top, but I smiled anyway. After I was out, he went to retrieve our overnight bags from the trunk.

Looking up, I noticed both my parents standing on the porch waiting for us.

I moved quickly toward them, and they surrounded me in the best hug together.

"Honey, we are so glad to see you." Mom was getting teary-eyed already. She had always been an emotional parent, but after Eli died, she got even worse. Mom and Dad stayed together instead of continuing with the divorce. They weren't wild in love anymore like they used to be, now they were just like roommates who already knew each other's lives and secrets.

"Mom, Dad, I'd like to introduce you to Dorian." I pulled back so they could say hello.

Mom looked at him, her reddish-brown hair framing her face, eyes so similar to mine. Everyone said my smile came from my dad. I was tall like him, and he had put on a little weight, but his brown hair was trimmed nicely, and his blue eyes were giving Dorian a strange look.

"Welcome, Dorian. Thank you for driving our daughter to us, that was very kind of you,"

Mom spoke first; Dad was sizing Dorian up. I found that pretty comical for some reason.

"It was my pleasure. Someone's gotta take care of our girl." Dorian's arm wrapped around my waist and pulled me in tight. Our girl. If that wasn't a declaration, then I don't know what was.

"Oh, Esme, you did good." Mom winked, and I knew my cheeks were turning pink. I wanted to shout out that we weren't together, but I bit my lip instead.

"Well, let's get these two lovebirds out of the cold, shall we, Sherry?" Dad gestured for us to follow, and we all walked into the house one by one, Dorian's hand stayed firmly fixed on my lower back as we did.

Chapter Eighteen

Esme

We had a nice brunch, and surprisingly, Dorian talked to my parents. He wasn't all silent and serious like usual. He smiled, he joked, and he touched me every chance he could.

I didn't wanna like it, but I kinda did. I kept telling myself over and over that it wasn't real, that as soon as we left my parents we would be back to screwing and that was it. No fake relationship. But every time he touched me, and every smile he threw my way, made my heart speed up.

Panic rose inside me as it dawned on me what was happening.

"Excuse me!" I jumped up from the table and all but ran to the bathroom.

I washed my hands and tossed some water on my face while I was at it. When my eyes met my own in the mirror, I saw something I didn't want to see.

"Don't you dare start to like him, Esme. He's bad news, and he doesn't have a heart to give you."

Oh God, I wanted his heart?

That couldn't be right. He was Dorian, asshole extraordinaire! There was nothing to make me fall for him.

Except the touching, and when he brought me expensive dinner, and stayed with me while I slept then carried me to bed, and when he came back to work to check on me after the explosion.

This realization hit me like a punch to the gut. I sat back on the covered toilet and digested all of these feelings. Dorian had been showing me kindness—not with words, but with his actions. His words were as sharp and cold as ever, but he had been taking care of me.

I felt so confused, not knowing what to do.

The tug of war between my mind and my head didn't stop after I left the bathroom, and in fact only got worse when Dorian leaned in to kiss my cheek when I sat back down at the table.

My eyes met his for a few seconds, and I wished it could be real. That I could let myself fall for him, and he wouldn't break my heart. Because he would. I don't think he knew any other way to be. But for that moment, when his brown eyes were staring into mine, I had a new wish.

After brunch, Mom wanted to take a short nap, saying she wasn't feeling well, and Dad decided to join her. Dorian and I went up to my old room. It was pretty normal as far as bedrooms go. I didn't have embarrassing teen heartthrob posters everywhere; I was more of a color girl, so my room was just colorful.

"You wanna talk about why you ran away from the table?" Dorian sat down and removed his boots and opened the top button of his shirt. Hello, sexy skin.

I walked over to my cork board of pictures on the wall and looked at the pictures of high school. Good times, old friends, and Eli.

"I'm confused."

I had been debating whether or not to talk to him about my feelings the whole way up here. I decided I should put it out there, so we could put an end to it before it got worse.

"Confused?" Now he was confused.

I turned around and leaned against the wall, next to those pictures of my past.

"I like you, and I think that after this trip, we should end this when we get home." There, I said it. His face scrunched up in confusion more. Yeah, join the club.

"You like me?"

I nodded.

"For some stupid reason, my heart beats fast when you're around. I wish I could control it, but I can't."

Oddly, my admission didn't make me want to be swallowed up by the earth. I'd accepted that I had feelings for Dorian despite the fact that he would most likely never have them for me.

"I'm not the good guy, Esme. I'm not going to change for you." His words were almost chastising, like I was a child that didn't know what I was doing.

"I know."

I held my ground, I didn't expect him to be someone other than who he was.

"That's why we have to end this before I fall harder and can't recover."

Dorian's gaze was burning into me. I prayed he understood what I was feeling. That pitter-patter in my heart kicked up when he stood and slowly walked over toward me, his face mere inches away from mine.

"I'm not letting you go," he stated, and I didn't know what to say.

"Dorian, I can't do this with you. It'll break me...I know it." I was pleading with him to understand, but his hands wrapped themselves around my waist, and his breath caressed my cheeks. This was too much.

"Please do the right thing and let me go."

One more plea, one more chance for fate to change course.

"I'm not letting you go," he whispered.

The moment before his lips touched mine, a sense of foreshadowing settled in my gut. Things would not end well for us. I knew it deep inside, like a knowledge I was born with. As he finally kissed me, hope replaced that dread. I may not be able to work a miracle with Dorian's heart, but if my own saw him worthy, then I guess I would go down in flames trying to prove it right.

Chapter Nineteen

Dorian

My hand caressed her soft skin while she slept peacefully against my chest.

I should let her go; it would be the best for both of us. But I wasn't ready to give up her taste and touch. She was addicting, and I didn't want to be without my fix.

Her future wasn't set yet. Every time I looked, there wasn't one where she got what she wanted and I got what I wanted.

There were two futures Phillip was playing his games for, and I wished I knew which. One seeming more likely than the other—easier. The other was a very dangerous bet to take. Everything had to line up, and he would have to wager on lives. He didn't have that in him; I'd had centuries of anger and practice to have that coldness when it came to playing with people's lives.

I looked down at Esme.

She was falling for me. Not a bright woman, to do something stupid like that.

Her pleas for us to end this between us fell on deaf ears. I wasn't done with her. I'd warned her before—I wasn't the good guy.

After our kiss, I carried her over to the bed and showed her exactly why we weren't over after this little trip. We moved and groaned into necks while chasing our own version of euphoria.

Something inside her had changed, and instead of the fight she'd been giving me lately, I saw hope. I didn't know what she was up to, but we both knew she wouldn't change me. She was fighting a battle she would lose.

Thirty minutes later we were back with her parents, chatting about hospital stories and embarrassing tales of Esme's past. When they talked about Eli, the whole room chilled. Sadness crept in, and it was obvious the family hadn't moved on from his death years ago. Esme would change the mood from dark to light quickly. I noticed that about her lately—she was like a little ember in the darkness.

But even embers could be put out.

When her parents called it a night, we retired to her room as well, having another bout of quiet fucking so we wouldn't wake her parents. It was odd, acting like teenagers who didn't want their parents to hear them messing around. I'd never had that experience growing up.

But then again, things had vastly changed since I was a teenager.

Esme stirred in her sleep, and her arm with the golden vein flopped over, giving me an up-close view.

I'd seen it many times, but never gotten to study it like this.

It was shorter than a few days ago. She'd healed someone recently. My bet was on her unsuspecting mother, who was coming down with something. It was flu season.

My unpinned hand reached out and gently ran a finger along the line.

I wonder why she didn't save her brother. They were old enough to have gotten their powers. She could have healed him instead of losing him, and I couldn't figure out why she chose to let him go.

She was becoming a puzzle that I wanted to piece together, but I had no time for that.

Taking a deep breath, I allowed myself to sleep with her against my chest.

The nightmare that was my worst memory started like it always did, and I knew I couldn't do anything but watch it all play out.

The dead were everywhere...brothers and sisters, my demigod family.

I bent over to check each of their necks for a pulse, but there was none—destroyed by the hands of their brethren and parents.

When I saw the form of Jasmine, I fell to the stone-covered ground and wept. She'd been like me, a good child of the gods. We had used our powers to help mankind. There was not a corrupt bone in her sweet body. We'd been together for a short time, but I'd fallen hard, and so had she. We talked over working in the temples of healing, helping mankind with our gifts. I'd always been a skilled healer thanks to my father, so naturally I would be wanted there.

I remembered seeing our futures together. Marriage, children, and dying together in our bed.

Never would I have thought demigods would turn on their own kind. But they did. And those who had survived the madness were slaughtered by those who gave them life.

I tried to find Jasmine. I'd been in my garden, concocting a tonic for us to drink that would mirror death. We'd escape the killings together. But she had gotten lost in the fray, and I was cornered in the temple. I drank alone and was dead in the eyes of those who were there to kill me.

When my eyes opened groggily, I searched for her, but to no avail.

Until now.

The sight before me made my knees give out.

I crawled across the rivers of blood and cradled her lifeless body in my arms.

"My sweet Jasmine, may your soul find peace in the fields of Elysium." I kissed her forehead, not caring that my lips were coated with the blood that was smeared across her head and soaked into her hair. She deserved better than this.

I held her for many minutes before going about making a pyre for my love and my fellow kind. They all deserved more than to be left dead on the ground.

I wished I could have done better, but I did what I could. After using wood from the homes of the dead and carefully collecting their coins, each body was ready to burn, the money to pay the ferryman over their eyes.

My eyes gave Jasmine's body one last glance before setting the wood to flames.

There were no more tears shed for the futures that were now burning.

Turning my back on what was, I grabbed the pack I'd made and walked away.

After weeks of traveling I'd found work as a healer in the army, under General Draco. He was said to have the blood of Achilles running through his veins and was unmatched in battle. We hadn't met before, but I tended to his men, getting them back to their feet.

It wasn't the life I had wanted, but it would do. Until that day I saw something that changed me.

My father, standing next to the other gods, next to Draco.

I hid behind a tree, praying that my father wouldn't be able to feel I was alive, but he never even glanced my way.

Then it dawned on me—they looked sick. They were dying.

Killing their own children hadn't sat well with mankind. Which led to the people giving up belief and faith in them, hence the dying. They couldn't live without people believing in them.

Served them right.

With one last chance to save the humans they loved more than their own blood, each of them spoke to Draco and told him that he was their chosen one to protect man. Their powers would be sent into the blood of mortals, who would need him to train and lead them.

My blood was burning as I listened to their words.

He slowly removed his armor and shirt, turning, giving his back to them, and sinking to his knees.

One by one, they sliced into their palm and touched his spine.

My mouth fell open in pure shock.

Once the last god burned his blood and power into Draco, they disappeared.

I couldn't believe what my eyes had shown me.

The gods had made Draco immortal, destined to carry out their will to protect mankind after having exterminated the demigods.

All except me.

Chapter Twenty

Esme

I loved seeing my parents, but I was happy to be heading home. They could only keep up the smiles for so long before the worried looks grew on their face.

So many emotions were running through my head that once Dorian drove us onto the highway, I pretended to sleep so I would have time to think in peace.

Nothing had changed in Dorian's eyes, but so much had evolved in mine. Even after we'd had sex, he touched me gently, and even held me while we slept. Somewhere deep in there, I had to believe he was capable of love. It was either that or get a restraining order because I didn't have the ability to push him away when he was near me. My heart and body refused to let him go. I just wished my mind was on their page in the book.

I knew we were going on the bridge to Seahill when the car slowed down to a near stop. Traffic sucked.

"You can stop pretending to sleep now," he announced, and my eyes flew open, staring at his in the reflection of the window.

Instead of moving or trying to defend myself, I stayed snuggled up against his seat facing the window silently.

"Going to ignore me forever?" he teased, and I rolled my eyes. I wished.

"I can admit you being silent has its advantages. No more mouthing off at me anymore, and I can just tell you what to do at work without a retort."

Yeah, I knew he was baiting me, and it worked. I turned over and leveled him with a look that promised he was going to regret his words.

"There she is. Being the silent mouse is not becoming of you anymore."

"I hate you," I huffed and wanted to say more, but we still had another half an hour of our ride together.

"We both know that's not accurate anymore. I'm pretty sure you said you were falling. Quite a tragedy."

"Yeah, well, maybe that fight you seem to like so much will be put to good use and fight this." I wanted to stick my tongue out at him, but I didn't.

"Or you can entertain me with your other thought of making me fall for you in return. Impossible but would be amusing to watch."

He did not just say that.

"Right now, I'm thinking murder would be easier."

"You wouldn't murder a cockroach." It was his turn to roll his eyes.

"You're not a cockroach; you're more like a mosquito, and I will kill one of those suckers in a heartbeat."

Yeah, I said he was like a mosquito.

"Interesting choice of creature," he stated while trying to figure out why I'd say that.

"You suck the life out of people, and you're annoying as hell." I felt pretty proud of myself for coming up with that, and he looked at me for a moment then laughed.

Why did his laugh have to make him seem so normal and attractive?

"What do you want, Dorian?" The words were out just as I thought them. I'd been wondering that all day. What did he want in life?

His laughter stopped sadly, but that was my doing. He wouldn't look at me as he spoke, and I found myself staring at his profile.

"Retribution."

I was not expecting that one word, but I knew it was deep. He had shared something very personal with me.

"And after that? Do you want to be alone until you die?" I couldn't stop asking these questions, wanting to understand him more. I guess he was in the giving mood because he answered me once more.

"I'll sit back and watch. Being alone makes no difference to me now." His voice was low, and while he didn't seem upset by my questions, I could tell he was struggling with these words.

"No family? Just being the famous doctor until you retire?" I knew I was pressing my luck with him, but I wasn't stopping.

"Family makes you weak. I'm never weak," he replied, and those words were harsher than the ones before. He was done. So instead of interrogating him, I talked about my dreams.

141

"I always dreamed of being a nurse part-time while raising kids with the love of my life. Loving strong. Maybe having a dog or pet. A decent house, not too large because then I would have to clean a big house. But we'd be happy no matter the size of the house, or the jobs we had, as long as we had each other." I smiled, thinking about that future, and hoped it could still happen for me. But I knew it wouldn't. Not just because of who I was falling for, but because I didn't want to die, leaving grief in my family. I'd seen what it did to people, and I couldn't do that to those who loved me.

Dorian didn't say anything for the rest of the drive to my apartment.

He parked in front of the building and got out to grab my bag.

"I'll see you at work," I said and reached up to kiss his lips briefly before turning to go inside.

Finally, I was alone.

I unpacked my bag and threw the clothes in the hamper, then made some tea.

With my steaming cup in hand, I settled on my bed and looked out the window to the cityscape before me. It wasn't a glorious view like many paid millions for, but it was enough for me. It was of the hospital, and the buildings behind it.

Tonight, I'd have to work, and I would see Dorian again.

I thought about what I wanted to do, and how I wanted to act.

The more I thought about it, the more tired I felt. I just wanted to be myself and do what I wanted. Live as I wanted. I lay down and took a short nap before getting ready, going through my routine of covering up my golden vein, slipping into scrubs, and walking over to work with a feeling of peace inside me. I would just be me. No more fretting over guarding my heart. That ship was waving to me as it passed by now anyway. And I really didn't want to end things. Who knew where they were going, but for now I was going to live my life to make myself happy for as long as I had left.

Chapter Twenty- One

Esme

"You look sexy." I leaned up to kiss Dorian's cheek in front of the nurses' station before walking away to see my next patient, an elderly woman named Barbara.

She was a frequent ER patient. Her husband had died a few years ago and I think she came in more for comfort than anything.

"Miss Barbara, what did I tell you about picking fights with stairs? The stairs always win." I smiled in greeting and went over to check her vitals.

Barbara was a petite woman in her early seventies, with short brown hair and green eyes. She was sweet as can be, but you didn't want to get on her bad side. She said things like they were to whoever.

"I know it. The little dog just ran next to me, and I tripped on the last few stairs trying to avoid him. Hopefully nothing is broken. I have my last grandchild's wedding this weekend to go to."

I knew she had fractured something, not horribly, but she was going be out of commission for a while.

I knew I shouldn't have done it—broken bones were easy enough to heal. But the heartbroken look on Barbara's face did me in.

"Well, we're going to get some X-rays to take a look, and we'll go from there." I placed my hand on her leg and pushed my power into her. She wouldn't feel much of anything right now, since it said on the record she had taken something for the pain. When the X-ray came back as normal, she would only feel a bruise. Just the bone would be healed.

While I waited for radiology to do their thing, I checked on a few other patients then went back with Dorian to give Barbara the results.

She always liked to ruffle Dorian's feathers, and I enjoyed every moment of it. A little old lady giving him a hard time, and he never really gave it back to her, which I always found surprising.

"Well, Ms. Barbara, it seems you are fine besides some bruises here and there. Just rest, ice, and try not to fall down anymore stairs." Dorian checked her over just to be sure she was okay then wrote some things down for his notes.

"Thank you, Dorian. With that out of the way, I think you two have some explaining to do." Dorian and I both looked at the woman with confusion on our faces.

She gave us a knowing look and shook her head.

"My eyesight may be going, but I can see what's happening in front of me very clearly. You two are in love. I always knew it was going to happen sooner or later." She smiled and reached over to touch my hand, giving it a little squeeze of approval.

Neither one of us said anything to deny or confirm her thoughts.

"Well, I hope to see this pretty lady on your arm in the newspaper pictures about that fancy function this weekend, Dorian. Call it a wish from an old lady. I could die any day, you know."

Oh my God, this woman is relentless.

"Put your worries to rest, Barbara—she's already on the list as my plus one." He was smooth-talking her, and I tried not to let my face show that I was in shock. She winked at me and then said she was all set.

After we were done making sure she was good to go, I pulled Dorian into the empty room next to Barbara's and closed the door behind me.

"What the hell, Dorian?"

He was looking up at the sky as if asking for heaven to grant him mercy. When he looked back down at me, he shrugged.

"I'm being honored at the hospital charity event this year, and now you're coming with me. Especially since you've made this between us public in the hospital."

I didn't have a fuck to give on that one. I was never afraid of what people thought of me, and I was tired of hiding things with him. But going to one of the hospital's big events was a huge deal. They were fancy, and the plates at the table were like a thousand dollars each. Every bigwig in Seahill would be there—even Phillip.

"I don't think I can go. I mean, I think I'm working that night, plus I don't have anything to wear, especially nothing that fancy."

"These really aren't things to stress about." He looked at his watch, and I knew he was busy, but was staying in the room for this moment while I was freaking out.

"I can't take off time like you can. I have bills, and I definitely can't afford an outfit for the event." I didn't like admitting my financial situation to him, but this was an immediate concern. He's seen my small apartment, so he should know I couldn't afford it.

"One night off won't make you poor, and I'll buy your dress. You can pay me back by telling everyone I'm not your boyfriend and that we aren't dating."

I wanted to laugh, so I did.

"I'm pretty sure everyone knows that we are just being intimate. You have a reputation of screwing nurses around here. Now I'm just another pin on your white coat." I rolled my eyes.

"I haven't slept with anyone here. Don't fuck where you work. It's bad for business. Like right now, I have to go." He started to leave, and I grabbed his arm, not letting him get too far. He looked down at my gripping hand and then up to my eyes.

"I'll go with you." I situated my body to fit in front of his and stretched up to kiss his lips, which quickly turned into a frenzy of passion and need.

"I'm coming over tonight, wear something I can rip off with my teeth." He pulled back and groaned. I wanted more of his lips, but I knew he had to leave.

We separated, and he gave me one last look of pure desire before leaving me in the room alone.

The rest of the night, I was in a perpetual state of happiness. Dorian may not see it, and wouldn't admit it, but we were dating, just without the formalities. His actions and his words just needed to find common ground on the subject.

Chapter Twenty-Two

Esme

Dorian had come by a few hours after I'd gotten home and found me waiting for him in the only lingerie I owned: a purple, lacy negligee.

To say he liked it would be an understatement. We hadn't even closed the door for two seconds before he was on me, and we were on the floor, not caring that we didn't even make it to the bed.

Afterward we were both tired from working all night, so I told him he could crash just to take the edge off before heading to his place if he wanted. Reluctantly he agreed, and we fell asleep quickly in bed together. My heart melted more for him, and he didn't even know it.

The need to pee woke me up from a really good dream about being on the beach. There had been puppies everywhere. Really, it was the best kind of a dream a woman could have.

I opened my eyes to see I was the only one in the bed.

Figures.

That need to use the bathroom was stronger now that I was awake, so I hopped out of bed and went about my business.

My appearance in the mirror was sort of scary, but since it was just me in the apartment, I didn't care. The bed was calling me back to it, and I planned on sleeping for at least four more hours before getting ready for work.

I was lying on my back and snuggling into the covers when a bright light flashed in my bedroom and then was gone.

What the hell?

Looking to where the light had come from, a loud gasp flew out of my mouth.

Dorian was standing there, wearing a blank expression on his face like he didn't just show up in my room like a flash bomb.

I didn't even know what to say, and he said nothing. He just stood there, waiting to see what would happen.

I did the only thing that came to mind: my fingers gripped my pillow and I threw it hard at his face.

"What the hell, Dorian?"

So many thoughts were streaming through my head that I couldn't even catch one to follow.

He caught the pillow before it hit and tossed it back on the bed then scoffed at me.

"Like you're one to talk, little miss healer. You should really stop healing everyone, by the way. You're not going to last long if you keep it up."

I couldn't move. Hell, I felt like I couldn't even breathe.

He knew I had powers? Not just any powers, but he knew in detail about *my* powers. What dimension did I wake up in? Dorian didn't have powers—unless being a jerk was a superpower, but I doubted it.

"How did you know?" I don't know why I did it, but I pulled my comforter up to cover myself, like a shield of sorts. I'd always kept it covered, and any healing I did I made sure no one could trace to me.

"I've never lied and won't now, but you don't want to hear the truth, Esme." His gaze was burning into mine, willing me to just accept those words and be done with this conversation, but I couldn't let it go. I felt betrayed, even though I'd kept my powers a secret too.

"How did you know about my powers?" I had to know.

"I have seen your vein and can smell the Fates on you. It's a lot more potent when you are around the sick and injured. You control their destiny." His face gave nothing away. He could smell the Fates on me? Like THE Fates? So, Eli and I had been right all those years ago. There were so many questions, and my head started to hurt from all the thoughts that were trying to come out.

"How do you know what the Fates smell like?"

"I used to know them."

He used to know them. The Fates. The fucking Fates of Greek mythology.

"That's not possible." I shook my head; it couldn't be true. There was only one immortal, according to Draco, and that was him. He would know about someone else.

Then it dawned on me.

The bright light, being old enough to remember the scent of the Fates. The way everyone at the society reacted to Dorian in a negative way.

Oh my God.

153

"It's you. I heard them talking about the man of light and having been there all along, but they never said who it was. It's you."

I couldn't believe it. Dorian was the man fighting against the Hero Society, and they kept it from me. Both of them. I was caught in a web between the heroes' omissions and Dorian's.

"You need to leave," I said coldly.

"I told you who I was, and you let me in anyway." He took a step closer, and my heart started beating faster.

He hadn't lied to me about who he was, just left so much out. He had always said he wasn't the good guy, but I never thought he meant he was the actual villain of Seahill. Leave it to me.

He kept moving toward me, his eyes staring into mine.

"Get out."

"No."

I wasn't a fighter, so when my hand slapped his face when he came closer, he looked shocked that I had hit him.

"Your mind knew I wasn't good for you, but you fell anyway. I even warned you, but you pushed me. I told you I'm not letting you go, and I'm still not. You're mine."

I went to smack his face again and he caught it mid slap.

His head started to descend, and I knew as much as I hated him right now, I loved him more.

I'd fallen in love with the bad guy, and that scared the hell out of me.

Chapter Twenty-Three

Esme

My heart picked up its rhythm, even though I didn't want it to.

"You know nothing has changed in your heart. I'm still the asshole you chose to care about." His lips moved down my jaw and to my neck.

My body responded to his touch, but I didn't let it show.

He knew anyway, though...how could he not, after all the times we've been together?

"I don't even know who you are!" My voice was hoarse. I really hated myself right now.

"I'm yours."

I started crying.

There was no stopping the outburst of tears that flooded my eyes and the tremors that shook my body. All of the emotions were too much, and I couldn't hold it together.

His face pulled back from my skin, and his hands cradled my cheeks, making me look into his eyes.

"I'm not capable of love; that part of me died a long time ago."

"Dorian, please." I didn't know if I was pleading for him to love me or for him not to tell me anymore. I wanted both and neither at the same time.

"You're beautiful." He leaned in and kissed the tears that were streaming down my face, which of course only made me cry more.

When his hand let go of mine to curl around my waist, I didn't put up a fight. I had none in me right now. Too many emotions had been brought to the surface, and I was incapable of doing anything until they ran their course.

Dorian held me on the bed while I let it all out and spoke to me about himself—words I'd yearned for but never thought I'd hear.

He told me of his power to manipulate light, using it to travel even great distances in an instant. Then he told me about being immortal. He never said how he was immortal, if that was a gift or not.

A man that was pure evil—as I'd come to think of the villain of Seahill—would not hold a woman and let her cry until she had nothing left in her but to close her eyes and let the silence of sleep welcome her.

Dorian was gone when I woke up to the sound of my alarm.

I should have called out, but I didn't.

I should have avoided Dorian, but I didn't.

My mind was in a complete state of confusion. I was in love with him, and we both knew it. He said he wasn't capable of love, but his actions were speaking differently, which made everything even more muddled.

Dorian kissed me once in front of everyone during our shift, but I'd managed to leave once it was done, and instead of going home, I headed toward headquarters.

I got a block down the street when I stopped and stared at the stars above.

They had all hid the truth from me.

They were my friends—family, even—and they didn't warn me about Dorian. They didn't know I was with him, but they could have said something, and they didn't.

Instead of heading to headquarters to demand answers, I walked the few blocks over to

Grand Bay Park. I sat on the wood bench and looked out at the water, so calm it was like glass.

"I'm sorry."

I should have known he would come.

"I don't know what to feel right now." It was as honest as I could get, and there was no use speaking anything but the truth to him anyway. My head turned to see Phillip all bundled up with a sad look on his face.

I turned my gaze back to the still water and felt the warmth of his body as he sat on the bench with me.

"You had to fall for him," he said, his voice full of regret. I didn't say anything, and he took that as my okay to continue.

"You're the only chance we have. It was a gamble, but I know love. I know the love you have for him is enough to be made into legend. It will be if you have faith in it, Esme."

I shook my head. This wasn't the love of legends I'd wished for. This was a tragedy of legends. Destined to love the villain and either lose him or lose humanity.

"The others didn't tell you because I told them not to. You are one of our family, and they care for you. They've tried to protect you, but your heart couldn't be guarded. You're the only one who can change him. Forgive them, Esme. Hate me, but forgive them." He sounded so heartbroken that I couldn't help but look at him.

His cheeks were pink from the cold nipping at them, but there were distinct tear stains down his face.

"I don't hate you." I sighed and then scooted closer to wrap my arms around him. He hugged me tightly, and we stayed embraced in each other's warmth for a few minutes.

"What do I do now?" I wished I had his power of sight. Then I would know my path and could follow it without doubting my every move.

"Live hard and love strong, Esme, and always have faith in that love."

I didn't say anything after that. My mind and heart were trying to accept his words as we watched the sun rise over the calm sea, which had started to ripple from a gentle wind.

Was my love for Dorian enough to change his heart? I didn't think so, but I decided to listen to Phillip and choose faith. It was either faith or be destroyed.

My fate had been decided the moment I gave myself to Dorian. I knew it then, and I knew it even more so now. My only chance was staying the course and having faith it was all going to work out the way it was meant to happen.

Chapter Twenty-Four

Esme

I was tired after having sat in the park with Phillip into the early morning hours, and all I wanted was a hot shower then sleep.

But all my thoughts went out the window when I saw a large black box sitting on my bed wrapped with a satin bow on top.

My apartment was locked, just like I left it, so I knew it was from Dorian. He had used his power to flash in and leave this.

My fingers were slow to open the box, feeling the softness of the ribbons before peeling off the lid.

Oh my.

Inside was layers of chiffon. He'd bought me a dress for the event tomorrow night.

I reached in to grab the bodice and held it up to my body. It was an off-the-shoulder, whimsical dress, that would be snug around my breasts and waist, then flowed out toward my feet. Attached to the bodice were very loose sleeves that stopped at my elbows. The color was a grayish blue and white, like the sky on a stormy day. The dress looked like a bohemian version of Cinderella's dress.

I noticed something shiny out the corner of my eye and looked over to see sparkling shoes sitting at the bottom of the box.

They were a simple style, but the outside looked like it was covered in little diamonds, giving it the appearance of being a glass shoe.

Well, seems I wasn't the only one who thought this looked like a hippie Cinderella dress.

I shook my head while walking to my closet and pulled out a hanger so this dress could breathe from the box. The material was so soft and fine. I'd never owned anything like that in my life. Dorian had money, and he'd lived a long time, so I'm sure he'd accrued it over the centuries. If he wanted to spend whatever ungodly amount he spent on this dress for me, then fine.

After a long shower, I curled up in bed and was just about to pass out when light flashed in my room, making my eyes squint together even more.

"I'm too tired to have sex," I muttered, not even opening my eyes to look at his face.

He didn't say anything, and for a moment I thought that maybe the bright light was something flashing from outside into my apartment, but then the bed dipped, and arms wrapped around me, pulling my body to lie against his chest.

"I like the dress, but I'm curious how you knew my size," I whispered while nuzzling myself against his apparently bare chest.

"I know every inch of your body. Knowing your size was no difficulty."

True. I guess that made sense.

I had one last question before I stopped fighting the sleep that was trying to grab hold of me.

"If you're the bad guy, why do you save lives?"

His body tensed, then relaxed a moment later. I guess he was surprised by my question.

"It's what I know. But things will be changing soon."

"Please don't," I whispered so low that I'm honestly surprised he heard me.

"I won't stop now. I've come too far." He shook his head and I didn't ask him anymore questions.

We slept together for hours, and then I felt him kiss me briefly before leaving the same way he came.

I woke up with hope inside my chest.

Dorian was falling for me, whether he knew it or not. I felt it deep inside my chest. There was no way he could hold me while I slept, buy me a dress that was perfect for me, and honestly not leave me when it would have been so easy to cut his losses, if he didn't care for me deeply. Especially with my ties to his opposers. He'd never asked me about them or tried to get me to play both sides. He only wanted my body, and that was it. Somewhere in our time together, he'd changed.

I got dressed quickly and went to work, hoping he was working tonight so I could kiss him and tell him officially that I loved him and had faith in that. That I wasn't giving up on being together. Ultimately, I was hoping he would choose love over his mission to destroy mankind.

Unfortunately, Dorian was off tonight, but I knew I'd see him tomorrow since I was his date.

Melissa Ann was sitting in front of the computer typing away when I arrived at the nurses' station.

She reached over to a small bag next to her keyboard and snatched some crackers before turning to look at me.

"Don't get pregnant, it sucks," she whined, and I laughed at her misery. She was starting to show a good bump, and I thought she looked adorable.

"Can't be that bad since you did it twice," I reminded her, and she rolled her eyes. Of course, I was right.

"So, you've managed to only kiss your hunk of burning love when I'm not on shift. I'm pretty disappointed you won't let me live vicariously through you and the doctor." She ate a cracker and gave me a sharp look.

"My apologies, I'll make sure to lay a big one on him the next time we're around you." I laughed, and she joined in with me.

I told her about the event tomorrow, and the dress he got me. I told her about how things have changed between him and me.

"I'm pretty sure anyone could have called it happening between you guys, except you two. You're the light to his dark."

She didn't know how much her words meant to me, and words wouldn't be able to tell her just how much I needed to hear them. So, I reached over and hugged her instead of speaking. I was the light to his dark, the star in his night.

I pulled back from the hug, and she gave a little squeeze before letting me go. We went back to laughing and talking about how much of a fool I was going to make of myself in front of all of Seahill's finest tomorrow evening.

Chapter Twenty-Five

Dorian

I told Esme I'd pick her up at five thirty, but I showed up early, not wanting to rush seeing Cinderella all dressed up for the ball. Truth be told, I'd already seen her in a series of dresses for the event, and none looked as good as the one I'd grabbed for her. Now I'd get to see it in person.

She opened the door shortly after I knocked, and I smirked. She wasn't ready yet.

"You're early!" She left the door open for me and ran back into the bathroom to finish dolling herself up.

I hope she didn't use that foundation shit. Her freckled skin was perfect without it.

After closing the door, I went to sit on her couch and wait for her to finish getting ready.

Not for the first time in the past hour, I started questioning what I was doing here, and what I was doing with her.

She didn't know everything, none of them did.

I'd underestimated her feelings, thinking she would push me away, but she hadn't. I could tell she was struggling with the person I was, and what I was planning to do, but she was still holding on for some reason. That was a lie in my head, and I knew it. There was a reason.

Love.

Love ruined lives. I'd seen it many times in my life.

It would most likely ruin her as well. But I was selfish and wasn't letting her go.

"Okay, I need you to zip me up! And don't get any ideas...I'm not messing anything up for your cock tonight," she called out from the bathroom, breaking through my thoughts enough to bring a chuckle from my lips.

I stood and walked toward the room and felt my steps slow when I saw her bare back against the soft fabric. She looked like a goddess, standing in that small bathroom.

Instead of doing what she asked right away, my fingers reached out to touch her skin, moving up her spine and across her shoulders, then caressing her back down to the zipper.

"You could have given Aphrodite a run for her money," I leaned in and whispered against her ear. Goose bumps rose on her flesh, making me grin. Aphrodite had been beautiful, but her personality dimmed her beauty. Esme was beautiful on the outside and the inside. I shook my head, thinking to when I thought she wasn't worth a quick fuck.

So much time I'd wasted, when I could have been touching her, feeling her against my skin.

Once she was zipped, she turned to face me, and I frowned.

She looked divine, just as I knew she would. But there was something missing.

Without another word I flashed out of her apartment and appeared in my bedroom at my penthouse. There were three visions where I saw her wearing the necklace I'd bought her. Two of them were fine, but there was one that made me pause in giving it to her. It had a very low percentage of occurring, but even that small amount stopped me for reasons I dared not give thought to.

The memory of Jasmine's broken body came barreling through my head, and then anger replaced whatever I had started to feel with Esme's future.

She'd be fine; I had nothing to worry about because I wouldn't fail this time around. I gripped the box tighter and flashed back into her bathroom, but she wasn't standing there.

"I'm in here."

She was in her room, putting on those sparkling shoes when I came around the corner. When she looked up at me, there was no sadness or turmoil in those beautiful eyes. And she didn't question where I'd gone, which I found odd.

"You needed something else." I walked over and held the box out to her.

"You're not going to Pretty Woman me, right?"

I didn't know what she was talking about, so I gestured for her to open it, which she did gingerly.

"Oh God, Dorian," she gasped and was shaking her head no.

Without asking for permission to do so, I lightly held the heavy necklace and placed it around her neck, quickly fastening it.

There.

Now she was utterly exquisite.

The string of diamonds circled her elegant neck, accentuating her collarbones, and a large teardrop sapphire that was the size of a quarter hung just above her breasts.

"Perfect," I told her, and she couldn't stop touching the large jewel hanging against her skin.

"For a man who doesn't do relationships, you're really good at spoiling your woman."

My face scrunched up at her words. We weren't in a relationship. Not in the way she was thinking. I didn't know what we were, but it wasn't that. This wasn't going to lead to marriage and kids in a suburban home outside the city.

"Time to go, Cinderella, don't want you to turn into a pumpkin." I held out my hand to help her up and then led her to grab a coat so she didn't freeze to death on the way to the event at the planetarium.

The drive was quiet, and we stood for pictures together once inside. Esme was tense the whole time, not used to the attention and all of the lights flashing, but she handled it well, smiling at the appropriate times, all while trying to rush through the area. I wasn't fond of the process myself, but since I was being awarded something tonight I needed to give them what they wanted.

It made the world trust that I was on their side. Once my plans became reality, that trust would all work in my favor.

We were stopped by many people once inside the large room with the elegant glass ceiling. Too bad the light from the city was too bright to see the stars that were usually breathtaking in the darkness.

Esme's whole body sagged when she spotted her friends in the distance.

"Go," I leaned in to tell her, while I talked to a man whose name I'd already forgotten.

Draco, Rose, and Phillip all stood by their table and were chatting when Esme came over. Rose hugged her tightly, and then started squealing about her dress and jewelry. They both looked beautiful—Rose was in a yellow dress that was sheer along her arms and flowed down to her toes. When she turned to talk to her brother, I could see there was no back to that dress.

Phillip looked strangely out of sorts, not with his usual confident swagger.

Then my eyes collided with Draco's. Instead of the sneer my body wanted to react with, I gave him a smirk. I was in control of this game, and he was waiting for me to mess up. The brute wouldn't have any issue strangling the life out of me right here in front of everyone, if he was allowed. But he wasn't. I was too important for him to act out his desires.

Moving my gaze away from him like he was nothing, I faked giving my attention to the man in front of me that was still talking even though it was obvious I didn't care about a word he said.

I excused myself when it was time for us to be seated. Esme was already walking over to me, and together we sat with some famous person, his wife, and the director of the hospital we worked at, plus his wife.

Esme chatted with everyone, keeping up pleasantries while we ate, and I kept my talking short. I wasn't known for being particularly loquacious anyway.

I was called up to the stage to accept Seahill's Man of the Year award, and I took the crystal sculpture and said thank you before walking off the stage.

The music began again, and people started to move to the dance floor. I was willing to do anything to get out of sitting at that table again, listening to those people go on about their lives, knowing it was all fake.

Chapter Twenty-Six

Esme

Without any words exchanged between us, Dorian all but tossed his shiny award on the table and took my hand gently, wanting me to follow his lead.

He led us to the dance floor, where people were starting to swirl around like something out of a fairy-tale story.

He spun me out before pulling me back to his chest.

I wasn't a dancer, but I followed his movements, and we were floating across the floor with ease. I laughed, mostly at myself.

"Not too shabby." I was surprised that I hadn't tripped yet or stomped on his foot.

My eyes had been on him since he stood in my doorway earlier. Dorian was a god in a suit. Never thought I'd be attracted to a guy in a tux, but I was willing to say to hell with my words earlier about not wanting to mess anything up for his cock tonight.

"Not too shabby at all," I commented to myself with a half smile, and I closed my eyes for a moment, basking in this feeling of being with him, no other thoughts of what else was happening around us.

The music slowed down, and he pulled me closer, our movements decreased. He wasn't done dancing with me yet.

The beat was romantic, and we swayed together like we'd been doing it for years.

I found him looking up at the ceiling when I finally opened my eyes again.

"No stars tonight," I commented, and his head came back down to look at me with longing in his eyes.

"The night has always been my favorite time. The silence and the beauty are incomparable to the other phases of the day."

He was looking at me like I was the night sky he admired so much.

"The night is my favorite too. I like to sneak out to the rooftop at the hospital when I get a break during third shift," I admitted, watching a grin on his face grow.

"Me, too."

I giggled, thinking about Dorian sneaking away from his busy job to stare at the stars, but this man was so complex, more than I could ever hope to know.

"I love you."

I couldn't hold it in any longer, so I was taking a leap of faith.

"You shouldn't. I'm too lost in the dark to feel your love."

"Then I guess I'll just have to leave my love in the stars, so you can find your way through the night."

My response had been quick, but it came straight from my heart. Dorian didn't think he could love, but I had faith that he could, he just needed to see the light for himself.

His mouth parted, obviously not knowing how to respond, and a small part of me hoped he would throw everything in his head out the window and kiss me. Love me, and never let me go.

But then his eyes snapped toward the door, and he moved quickly, leaving me on the dance floor alone.

Phillip was at my side instantly, and I looked to him for answers. Something was happening, something big.

Draco and Rose appeared moments later, and I didn't wait to hear what was going on, instead running to the doors Dorian had disappeared through in search of him.

I heard a commotion as soon as the cold air hit my skin when I pushed the doors open to the street.

All of the people who were out here earlier were gone—even the valet workers were inside staying warm.

"Dorian!" I called out. A feeling in my gut told me he was part of the commotion down the street. I took off running, not caring that Rose was calling after me to wait.

There were people shouting, and the energy was charged, with mad blood in the air ready to ignite and demolish the city.

The Hero Society stood on one side, and part of Dorian's crew I could assume stood on the other.

"What the hell is happening here?" Draco demanded as he walked onto the scene like the ancient general he was.

"They caught us by surprise, breaking into headquarters and locking us in the containment room while they trashed the place," Leon said, his lip dripping blood.

I didn't want to believe it was true, but I knew it was despite hopes and wishes.

Dorian was looking over one of his people and then flashed closer to my group.

"Our time to fight isn't now," he stated, then turned his back to us. It hurt, but I knew who he was and what part he had to play.

Draco was not giving up his chance to finally have Dorian in his grasp. I stood there silently as he lunged for Dorian, who avoided his movements with the fluid grace of a cat.

"He has sight, Draco, you won't win!" Phillip yelled, and my hand flew to my lips. Dorian had sight like Phillip did? Had he been planning for me to fall for him all along? My heart was hurting, and I knew it was only going to get worse.

Everyone stood there, watching their two leaders in an intense battle, immortal against immortal.

Someone had to stop them. Phillip grabbed my arm and wouldn't let me go.

"You get near him and he'll die," he warned me, and my lips parted. I didn't want him to die. I needed him to let go of the hate that he harbored deep in his soul and choose love.

Faith.

This was going to be okay. It had to be.

Everyone was completely enraptured by the scene before them.

Draco cursed and then spit blood from his mouth. They couldn't die—why would they keep fighting? This had to be personal on a level that we didn't understand.

"Dorian, please." I begged for him to stop, to choose me over this. He looked at me, and Draco used the opportunity to punch him hard in his perfect face.

Dorian smirked and then spit out his own share of blood.

Draco took a step back, seeming to be shocked by the blood on the pavement. It did look odd.

"Demigod," Draco cursed, and then looked at Phillip as if he knew this all along.

Demigod?

"It's impossible." Draco shook his head, not believing what he had discovered.

"I'm very much here, and I will have revenge!" Dorian shouted and then began to attack Draco with a fierceness I never imagined he possessed. Both men were lethal, and I was afraid for them. They were too evenly matched.

Someone from Dorian's team shook out of his shock and moved toward Leon so fast he was just a blur.

Then the others followed. Stolen powers fought the originals, and I couldn't help but fall to my knees at the sight before me. Brother fighting brother. Hate fighting hate. It had to end.

Draco and Dorian were covered in each other's blood splatters and still fighting, but both seemed to be losing energy quickly.

Leon and his battle partner were causing chaos with all the buildings around us, debris falling everywhere, and a light pole came crashing down behind Rose, Phillip, and me.

"We have to do something!" I looked back at Phillip, and he was standing there with a face that said it all. This was supposed to happen. He was following his line to the bright future he wanted for us.

I wasn't okay with that. Someone was going to get hurt, maybe even die. I couldn't let that happen. I wouldn't let it happen.

My legs found their strength, and I started moving toward the two men that were fighting for a death that neither could find.

Chapter Twenty-Seven

Esme

I was maybe five feet away when time seemed to slow, and I watched as Draco grabbed a piece of rebar that had fallen from all the debris around us.

"No!" I cried out as he moved it slowly into Dorian's chest.

Dorian's eyes were wide with shock as he let go of Draco's torn shirt and fell to the ground.

Red and golden blood flowed out past his lips, and I ran to him, pushing Draco out of the way.

The fighting around us stopped—every single person was still, watching the villain of Seahill struggle to breathe against the blood filling his lungs.

"No, no. Dorian!" I cradled his face while looking into his pain-filled eyes and then to his wound. He was dying. Dorian was dying. How could he die? He was immortal.

"Demigods aren't immortal. He's been on borrowed time for ages." Draco stood there, watching his foe slowly head toward the darkness that beckoned him. I didn't blame Draco for this, but I grieved that he hadn't seen what I had in Dorian.

Dorian's body gave away, and he collapsed on the ground with a loud thud.

His eyes were on me, blood coming out of his lips and the corners of his eyes.

"You can't leave me, Dorian. I love you. Please, baby, don't leave me. I have faith in our love; it's the kind I always wished for. The love of legends. Don't let this be the end, Dorian." I lay on the ground next to him and cried, pleading for him to miraculously pull through.

"Esme," he croaked and his eyes closed.

I looked to his chest to see it was still moving but barely. Dorian was on the edge of death.

"Not this time. I'm not losing another person I love when I can do something." I gave myself a pep talk before sitting up and reaching for the bar in his chest. I pulled, and pulled hard. Red and golden blood was pouring out of his chest when I finally freed the metal from his body. I placed my hands over his chest, feeling the liquid seep through the cracks in my fingers, and began pushing my power into him. I would not let him die.

His eyes opened suddenly, and he seemed to be choking, but I wasn't stopping.

My hands started glowing, a bright gold covering the wound in his chest. I glanced over to my vein and saw that it was losing its color fast. I realized that by healing him, I would be giving up what was left of my life, so he could live.

I should have thought about that more, but I didn't care. I couldn't live in a world where he wasn't. He would survive without me, but I would not without him.

Peace settled over my mind as I accepted my fate.

His wounds began to heal, but it wasn't enough. He needed everything I had, and I gave it to him.

"Esme, no. You're giving him too much," Rose shouted, and I shook my head.

"You can never give too much for love," I said out loud, but already I was getting weak.

Dorian's eyes never left mine, and I wished I could read his mind.

Did he feel my love healing him? Bringing him back to life with my last breath?

I could barely keep my hands up from the weight settling in my body, but I managed, lying down next to him.

"No," he managed to croak, but I just smiled weakly at him.

My power was gone, and with them my years of life.

I could feel the cold soothing my veins.

Dorian was healed and sat up to cradle me in his arms.

"Look to the stars and find my love in the dark," I whispered, reaching out to touch his face with my hand before it fell back against the cold ground.

Love and death surrounded me, and I was at peace. Looking up at the stars, I saw the darkness coming for me.

Then he was there.

"Eli," I whispered to my brother and let his light surround me, taking us home.

Chapter Twenty-Eight

Dorian

Rain.

It was raining that night when I first took Esme to her bed. I guess it was only fitting that it was raining at the end.

Stupid.

I wished I had the power to bring back life from the hands of death, only so I could tell her how stupid her decision was to end her life to save mine.

It'd been a week since that night.

A week since I watched her eyes gloss over and that bright light inside them vanish, while her last words called for her brother Eli, as if she could see him coming to retrieve her for the afterlife.

My eyes drifted toward the crowd opposite me, staring at the black casket between us.

They did this to her. The so-called heroes. The women were crying, and their men were consoling them as best as they could in the situation. Phillip was looking off into the distance, as he had been the whole time, not ready to accept his choices. He let her die. He saw it coming, as did I, and he straddled that line to make sure it happened.

For what future? The one where I would fall for her, and suddenly give up my fight against them? Join their team? He gambled wrong, and Esme paid for it with her life.

I was ready to die.

For centuries I'd trained, becoming a master at battle, so that one day I could best the infamous general of ancient Greece. But I failed.

He would always be the brawn in our fray.

But I was smarter.

A hand touched my shoulder, and I looked next to me to see a sobbing Melissa Ann trying to comfort me.

She was wasting her touch.

Esme was gone, and nothing could bring her back. No amount of comforting touches was going to change that.

Rage burned inside me, and my eyes landed on Draco.

They did this.

And they would pay.

She should never have been a part of their society; they should have left her alone.

I should have left her alone.

Everyone rose at the pastor's urging, and a young woman came up to the stand, bringing the microphone close to her mouth, singing out a song of being at peace, and celebration of parting ways.

Her parents cried together with the music, knowing they were burying their last child.

Esme had everything planned for her funeral, knowing she wasn't going to live that long if she kept using her gift. I knew she hadn't planned on this, though—falling for the villain. In the end, it destroyed her.

One by one, people walked over to her closed casket and placed an object on top of it. The thought was silly, especially since there was no taking materials with you after you died.

Still, when it was my turn to say goodbye, I couldn't help reaching into my coat pocket and pulling out the metal. I placed two obol coins from my ancient home over her casket, to pay her way across the river, even though it had long dried up.

I stared down, envisioning her wearing a soft blue dress, much like the one she wore to the gala.

My hand reached back down in my pocket and rubbed my fingers against the other item I couldn't bring myself to leave at home.

"You shouldn't have fallen for me." I pulled out the necklace she'd worn the night she died. Delicate and beautiful like the woman who'd worn it.

I placed it on the casket swiftly then stormed off without any words or glances to anyone. They weren't worth my time right now. I had plans to execute and retribution to collect.

Rage replaced my blood, and I had fuel to fight until the bitter end.

One way or another, the night I loved so much would blanket the earth, and darkness would reign.

Once I was out of sight, I flashed back to the mansion and ran into Jax.

He was sporting a black eye, and I wanted to give him another.

Without my orders, they'd gone into the heroes' headquarters and locked the crew in their containment room. Roady, our hacker, had bypassed their system in seconds. They thought they were helping, but they fucked everything up. My silence was punishment enough as I walked down the hall toward my room.

It was still trashed from that night Esme died. Pieces of wall littered the floor from all the holes and slices I'd made.

There were no fucks to give when it came to cleaning it up. None of it mattered.

Draco and Phillip scooped her right out of my arms and took her to the hospital.

I had been helpless to do anything, and their attempts to save her were pointless. She was dead.

After ripping off my funeral clothes, I went back to doing as I had been since that night: training. I had to be faster, more precise, and focused on my goal.

Hours passed the same way. I'd quit working at the hospital. It was wasting time that I could spend preparing.

The solar eclipse was just a few days away, a time when I would be at my height of power. The heroes wouldn't stand a chance of stopping me.

They tried to save me with love, and all they'd done was piss me off further.

Night was coming for them.

Chapter Twenty- Nine

Draco

"That's it. I can't be silent today. Not after everything I felt at that funeral." Rose was up on her feet, staring her brother down. We'd all been sitting in the chill room silently, everyone dealing with Esme's death in their own way.

"You told us not to tell her, and look what happened. She died! She died, Phillip." I didn't even need to see her face to know tears were falling down her soft cheeks.

Phillip said nothing, as he had since that night. The smile he normally wore had been missing ever since.

"You knew this was all going to happen, and you let it happen anyway. Who's next, Phillip? Who are you willing to let die for this future you've chosen for us? Me? Mina? AJ? Asher, and Echo, and Leon, and Lilith? Charles? Who, Phillip? One of ours is gone because we hid Dorian's role from her. She was in love with him, deeply in love. I felt it while she used her power to save his life. We could have prevented all of this. Hell, she had powers, and we never even knew."

She didn't mention my name because there was no way for me to die, even if I'd wished I could join them in death if they were there. Living without them—without her—would gut me.

Rose was desperate to end the pain and suffering that had taken over everyone. But she was just as helpless as I was. To use her powers to make others feel better, she would have to feel better herself, and that wasn't the case. Rose felt everything too deeply.

I tried to pull her back to sit in my lap, but she was out of my arms and standing in front of Phillip, who was looking at her with a tick in his locked jaw. He was in pain. Probably in more pain than any of us. I could see it, but she was too blind right now to understand his suffering.

The movement was fast, and every mouth in the room dropped as her petite hand sliced through the air and struck her brother across the cheek.

Instead of coming back to me, she left the room in sobs.

The rest of the crew sat there, trying to process everything. One by one, they all left to go grieve, leaving Phillip and me alone after Mina kissed his red cheek and walked out.

"It's not easy," I said, knowing what he was feeling right now.

His eyes collided with mine and he knew I understood.

"She was our only chance to make it all right." He was breaking, tears he hadn't let the others see were started to spill over his eyelashes.

"I don't wanna know the future. It's always been a cursed power, in my opinion, but I know what it's like to make sacrifices. It's never an easy choice, but someone had to make it."

I'd been red with rage when fighting Dorian. Centuries of pain had taken over, and I couldn't see anything but his end.

"The burden of her death doesn't lie solely upon your shoulders. It's mine and his, too."

I should have seen what was right in front of me. That something was powerful enough to make Esme choose her fate. Dorian should have seen it too—hell, maybe he did, but ignored it.

Whether he knows it or not, he loved her too.

I'd seen it in his eyes when she was gone.

It was the same look I gave Rose that moment when she had put herself in danger to save me. Love that could reach the stars.

I didn't know his history.

But being a demigod gave me a good idea. He was the only one of his kind. Everyone else had been put down one way or another. That in itself would stir and make even a sane man go mad.

Somehow, he'd known about me, and throughout history had been trying to sabotage me. He played his part well, though, I'd give him that. We had no clue until Echo pieced it all together. I'd read the files of his journal after that. His hatred of me was palpable, and he would stop at nothing to see me lose everything, just like him.

I'd seen the look on his face at the funeral. He was pissed to hell, and more focused than before to see the world end.

Let the freaks free, and the humans would become their playthings.

"It's only going to get worse," Phillip said, his hands covering his face in frustration. I knew the feeling. Everyone could feel the air shifting, turning dangerous, as if waiting for a spark to ignite it.

"Always feels this way before war."

The anticipation of what would happen, the fear that you could die, and the sadness knowing that you will probably lose those close to you...I would do everything I could to stop that from happening. No more loss, no more suffering. I stood, not sure what exactly I could do right now, but I had to start somewhere.

"Go home. He'll show up for a chat. He's not even blocking me on his moves right now. Teasing me of what he's capable of." Phillip gripped his hair tightly. The visions were haunting him. I walked over and put my hand on his shoulder in a comforting manner, then left for my truck without another word. He knew all I could say, but the touch said enough. Everyone was hurting, him included. They all needed their time, and then they would come back around.

The drive back to my demolished cabin was quiet, and the sun had finally gone down.

For a brief moment once I got out of my truck, I looked out at the city scape through the trees then back at my old home.

I did miss my quiet life.

I missed my chickens and my cows. I missed not having any responsibility but taking care of them and being in the darkroom. It was the easier choice, but not the right one.

The forest around me lit up, and I knew he was here.

There would be no fight. This was the calm before the storm, and my only hope at trying to fix this before war came.

Chapter Thirty

Draco

Dorian stepped into my peripheral view to my right.

He was staring at the city, his hands in the pockets of his dark denim jeans, looking casual in the winter air.

We were silent for a brief moment before I turned to face him fully.

"How?"

He knew what my question meant and kept staring off at the city.

"I drank a tonic that made me seem dead. When I woke, they were all gone. I'd served in battle as a healer, and witnessed the gods' end with you, *brother*." He looked at me and sneered at the word brother.

I'd been given a small amount of their blood, to seal the deal, a secret I'd kept even from the others. But Dorian and I shared blood—we were family, to some degree.

"Apollo?" I guessed. Light was Apollo's thing, plus the medicinal gifts. Dorian nodded.

"I wasn't a part of the demigods' demise," I told him, hoping he knew that I hadn't been there for that. At least to strike one thing on his list off.

"I know. You were the chosen one, while they killed their own children." His voice was calm, but his words told another story.

"I didn't want this—to live this long, to watch everyone I cared about die. Immortality isn't all it's cracked up to be, as you know." I glanced off toward the city, missing Rose. I hadn't checked on her before I left, knowing it would have conflicted her more with me there. She needed her own time right now, but I would see her soon enough.

"I won't stop," he told me, and I knew that would be his answer, but I had to try. Rage had been replaced with resolve, and all I wanted was to make things right.

"I'm sorry about Esme."

I gambled bringing her up, and by the way his body tensed, I had gambled wrong.

"She was nothing to me, and now she's dead. That boy bet on the wrong future," he hissed, and a shimmer of light started to appear around his body. He was going to leave.

"I know hurt; I know pain. If you don't face the truth, Dorian, agony will consume you like your hatred already has. We don't have to do this, brother. There's still time to right our wrongs." It was a Hail Mary attempt. I sent out a prayer to whoever in the universe was listening that Dorian would see reason and choose the right path, not the easiest.

His eyes leveled me with a glare of torment and pure rage.

"You know nothing of the pain I've felt, but you will soon."

Light started to encase him, and I knew there was only seconds left before he vanished.

"You didn't deserve her. You didn't deserve her love."

He was gone moments after the words left my mouth. I knew it would sting him, but we both knew they were true. She believed there was something more in him, and he was proving her wrong by continuing on this path.

Hell, her sacrifice fueled him more.

The world had barely survived demigods the first time, and now we had one that had thousands of years of anger built up, ready to be unleashed upon mankind. There was nothing stopping him now, not anymore.

But we would still fight.

I hopped back in the truck and drove to headquarters.

Rose was asleep when I climbed into bed at the apartment I was staying at above the restaurant. She was sleeping in my bed instead of at her apartment, just to be close in case anything happened.

She groaned and turned into my torso, moving her hands against my bare chest.

"I feel awful for hitting him," she confessed, as I knew she would. Rose was kind, but had that warrior's spirit in her. She lashed out in hurt and anger. Phillip knew it, but that crack of her palm against his cheek would echo in the room for days to come.

"He knows and understands, but can't change what is," I said as I wrapped my arms around her, holding her tightly.

"I don't wanna lose you," she mumbled against my chest, and I wanted to chuckle. She couldn't lose me—I was immortal. Before I could comment, she spoke the words I never wanted to hear come out of her mouth.

"I'd lose you if I died. I don't wanna die."

I spent the rest of the night telling her it wouldn't happen, that she would be protected, and Phillip wouldn't allow her to die, but I knew deep down that he would sacrifice everything. But if everyone was gone, what happy future would there be for us? I didn't know.

She needed a distraction, to not feel for even a few moments, so I gave her that—my body, my words—and she found peace for the night, resting in the safety of my arms in an orgasm coma, as she called it, having learned the phrase from one of her many romance books.

I was glad she still found time to curl up in her chair with a blanket, tea, and a book. Some people believe that you have to be happy all the time, but it wasn't true. I'd lived long enough to know that it was those little moment in the chaos of life that made us happier people. One minute of doing what you enjoyed is all you need to keep you going, sometimes.

Sighing, I closed my eyes and tried to feel the happy that was flowing from Rose's skin to mine. I felt heavy with everything that had been happening. But at least I had her with me. I had the Hero Society. I was blessed to have people care about me.

Tomorrow was a new day, and we needed to start preparing for what was coming.

Tonight, I would sleep well, with the woman I loved against my chest.

Chapter Thirty-One

Dorian

"You've lost, and we are free."

My battle cry bellowed throughout the city as Draco fell, sword to his chest.

He would heal, of course, but he would never truly live.

My army raised their fists in the air in victory.

My eyes landed on the dead below. I did give them a chance to join me, to give up their righteous Hero Society and just be free. It wasn't like I wanted to take over the world and become their king. I wanted people with powers to come into the sun, to be who they were meant to be. Not some superhero race who watched over mankind from the shadows.

"We won't ever give up. Remember that, Dorian," Echo called out. She was completely bare, her body covered in dirt and blood after having fought in her animal forms. Asher was by her side,

but there was blood rushing down his head. He
would survive. I'd seen it. So would she.

They looked down at their fallen comrades.
Phillip's sister was lying on the ground, eyes closed,
hands lying on her bleeding stomach where Draco
had placed them gently after she died.

Leon and Lilith were embraced together on
the grass. She had sacrificed herself to save his
good soul from going to hell, damning them both to
perish together. At least they had that.

Phillip rushed to Draco's side and pulled out
the sword in one quick motion, blood pouring out
from his wound. I hoped it hurt.

"You chose wrong, Griffin, and you lost
everything." I spared a glance at him, my words
laced with venom.

"You never deserved the love she gave you,"
he spat at me and lunged.

I fell back against my bed, tired from having
trained hard today. The vision was still the same,
after having checked through them again for the
tenth time today. The future I wanted was the
leader in probability. It was war, and in the end, I
would have my victory.

"You never deserved her," I scoffed aloud.
Everyone was making it a point to tell me that,

both now and in the future. I couldn't change anything, even if I could.

I shut down that thought because there was no point in entertaining it. Esme was better than me, and they were all right. I didn't deserve her love. I didn't want it. Told her that from the beginning, but she fell in love anyway.

My eyes closed, and I could still see her face. Time would go on, and I doubt I would ever forget the way her eyes would spark with fire when I pushed her. The way her lips parted without her knowledge when I wrapped my lips around her icing-covered fork.

Every moan she'd make when I was inside her.

"Dammit, Esme."

I cursed and sat up swiftly.

Every time I thought of Esme, all it did was piss me off.

No matter what I did, I couldn't stop thinking about her.

The way she looked at me tenderly when she pushed her power into me, healing me with her life force.

Look to the stars and find my love in the dark.

It wasn't her love I wanted, but that didn't stop me from flashing up to the roof of my mansion to stare at the dark sky. The clouds had been covering up the stars since she died, as if she took their light with her in the afterlife.

I knew nothing of what awaited people after death now.

Was the God that many believed in real, and had a heaven for them in the sky?

Or was there nothing, now that the underworld had no keeper, and the rivers had dried up?

A mystery that even stumped me.

The wind was cold, and bit against my cheeks, but I paid it no mind. I was used to pain, and so the chill was nothing to me.

I sat there for hours. Time was of little importance right now. So, I waited for an opening in the clouds, wishing I didn't know why I was there.

Truth was, I missed her, and looking at the stars was as close as I could get to her.

"I bet you're laughing at me now." I spoke to the wind as if it would carry my words to wherever she was. She liked watching me suffer in a non-dying way. Teasing me, showing me her backbone, and defying me.

"I could use your banter as a distraction." I laughed thinking about the bantering back and forth we did. That attitude.

"I could use some of your other special abilities now too," I mumbled, wanting to run my fingers through that thick hair of hers and then caress her creamy skin. The more I thought of her, the more I began to hurt.

I'd grown to care for her, that I knew.

The moment I hesitated in giving her that necklace I'd bought for her, I knew there was more than just a sexual attraction. I'd been in denial.

"It wasn't love. But it was something. You were something."

My head went down a dream that had never even been in the realm of possibilities. I'd fallen for Esme and could keep her. There was no Hero Society, there was no revenge in my veins. Just us. Fuck knew where that dream would have gone, but when that opening I'd been waiting for in the clouds appeared, I took the opportunity and wished on a star for what could have been.

"At least now you won't have to choose between your friends and me. You would have hated me no matter what. It's better this way."

I stood and felt my soul ache.

I was glad Esme was gone. She'd died with love in her heart for me, instead of dying from my hate.

"Goodbye, Esme," I said to the stars, just as the clouds covered up that gap.

They were all right—I didn't deserve her, but at least she didn't know that before she died, despite me telling it to her. She had hope, a false hope, but hope in us, nonetheless.

Leaving the roof, I went back to my room to train. It was the only solace I had left, until the heroes fell. Then, and only then, would I finally find peace in this hell.

Chapter Thirty-Two

Draco

"Again!"

Leon came at me with speed, and a fist that would knock a normal man out cold. But I moved slightly to the right, and he missed. I'd learned how to fight against his set of powers years ago, so today I was training with him to help learn to be a little less predictable.

The fight against the man who hosted his stolen powers had been getting to Leon's head. Since then he'd been wanting to know how to best someone like him. Both Lilith and I were giving everything we had, but ultimately it would come down to the other man's fighting. That and making sure Leon had a clear head.

He was still hotheaded at times, and stubborn. But he'd come a long way since he first joined our family. Lilith had moved in with him in the apartment above, and both were quick to respond in any situation and were enjoying their still-new marriage as best as they could.

I dodged his next few punches but then let him land a roundabout kick to my stomach after tensing for the blow.

"You need to anticipate where he's going to move next, not just think about where he is at that moment. Where will he go? You have to think two steps ahead. If he gets his arms around you, you're done for," I told him and moved on quick feet to catch him off guard. He managed to block me and then moved in a blur to my right, nailing me in the side with his fist.

"Good," I told him, and we kept sparring until Lilith came in and said AJ wanted to see Leon.

"Wanna wrestle?" Lilith smiled wide and waggled her eyebrows at me.

There had been a bet going as to which of us would win a fight against each other. We played around a few times sparring, but, in the end, I was only more lethal than she because of how long I'd been training. She was not far behind though.

"Rain check."

She winked at me and walked over to the weapons corner to throw some knives at a target, making a perfect heart shape around the bull's-eye.

My eyes looked over to Rose, who was jogging on the treadmill, with Mina sitting next to her on an exercise ball eating from a bag of pretzels. I walked over to grab my drink and sat on the mat to stretch out my aching muscles.

I'd been thinking about our future together lately.

The uncertainties of it all.

If by some miracle everything was fixed, and the upcoming war never came, we would live out her life together, and then she would die. I would be alone again.

She deserved the perfect future. Whatever job she wants, maybe in psychology like she went to college for. Maybe even get married and grow old with her husband. Have kids.

There was nothing in the world that I wanted more than giving that future to her. Immortality had always been a gift and a curse.

A gift because I lived long enough to meet my true soul mate, but a curse because one day I would outlive her.

I'd try though, to give her whatever she wanted. Even kids, if she desired. I didn't want her giving anything up for me if I could do something about it.

She glanced at me briefly and smiled before turning her attention back to her task of running while listening to Mina ramble on about whatever she was consumed with now.

I loved her smile.

Hell, I loved everything about her.

The more I watched her smile and laugh at Mina, the more I started to smile. She was still hurting from our loss, but she was my warrior, finding her happiness again.

Fuck it.

I hopped up and walked over to the girls.

My finger quickly pulled the emergency stop cord, making Rose stumble a bit from the change of pace, but I caught her and lifted her in my arms.

"Marry me, beautiful."

I should have probably picked a better way to propose to her, romantic and shit, but I couldn't stop myself from marching over here and blurting it out.

Her eyes were wide, and her arms gripped my shoulders as if she was trying to steady herself from falling over. I was holding her, so that last movement was strange.

"Draco, what are you—"

"I don't want to waste any more time without you being my wife. Be mine, Rose, in every way possible. My woman, my lover, my friend, and my wife?" I smiled and leaned in to kiss the tears that started falling onto her cheeks, spending extra time on the cheek with her beautiful birthmark, as I always did.

"But what about everything else going on?" She looked down at Mina, and a small expression of guilt passed over her face.

"Do you want to marry me, beautiful?" I asked, and she nodded.

"Of course I do, old man."

I laughed, and she was smiling from ear to ear, just the way I liked her to be.

"Then none of it matters. Let's get married."

"Probably a good idea before you get hard of hearing. Don't want you to miss hearing me say I do." She teased at my age as always, but it didn't deter me from leaning in to press my lips against hers.

"Maybe you should moan it to me; I hear your moans particularly well," I muttered against her lips and heard a groan next to us.

"You guys are too much. Honestly. I'm trying to eat here." Mina ate another pretzel then stood to congratulate us.

"A Hero Society wedding—first of many, I'm sure. Congrats, guys!"

Chapter Thirty- Three

Draco

It was amazing how quickly everyone put together a wedding for us.

Phillip had booked some fancy wedding barn months ago for this occasion, should it be the right one, which of course had made Rose squeal and give him a big hug. It was a start to mending the rift between them.

Lilith went into executive mode, designating people to get to work shortly after we told everyone. Echo and Asher showed up later, hugged us, and offered themselves up to do whatever we needed. I didn't care where we got married—I just wanted Rose as my wife.

It was an intimate wedding: our crew, plus Phillip and Rose's parents and grandparents. That was it. I had no true family besides them.

I stood beneath a snow-covered tree by the barn, wearing a tux for the first time. It was cold as hell outside, but Asher was pulling some magic that buffered us from the cold. Actually, it felt like spring outside to us, it just didn't look it. Everyone was dressed in stunning dresses and tuxedos, which for everyone except Phillip was like playing dress-up for the night. They all enjoyed it.

Then she stepped into my view.

Rose and I stared at each other as her dad walked her down the aisle. She was breathtaking, and she was really going to be mine.

She was a vision of beauty in a long-sleeved lacy top that cut off at her waist and a ball gown bottom. I wished I had my camera to immortalize this moment, her looking at me, accepting me, flaws and all.

I heard the clicking of the photographer Phillip hired and wanted to roll my eyes. Loud shutter button.

Rose smiled, and I grinned back at her. I'm sure she knew it was driving me nuts not being able to shoot this wedding for us. But I was the groom, and my hands would be full of my wife. No camera needed to make this moment better—it was already perfect.

Her dad kissed her cheek and went to stand next to her mother and the rest of our little crowd.

I didn't pay attention to what the pastor said, I knew the whole spiel. My focus was just on her, taking in every detail, searing it into my memory forever.

Of course, I couldn't stop myself from teasing her when she said "I do" with that sweet but mischievous look on her face.

"I'm sorry, could you repeat that? I'm kind of hard of hearing at my age, young lady."

Everyone laughed, and I could tell by Rose's face that she wanted to kiss the shit out of me. So, my first job as her husband was to enable that look.

"I do," I hastily said, and then, not caring about the parts that came after, my fingers lightly touched her cheek before taking that small step to close the distance between us.

Everyone and everything else around disappeared as our lips touched.

She had been mine ever since I had found her in my chicken coop. I'd fought it at first, but then gladly gave in. Now she was my wife, my world. There was nothing I wouldn't do for her.

Hooting and laughter filled the air around us, making Rose pull back with blush staining her perfect cheeks.

We were surrounded by hugs and congratulations in minutes.

Afterward we moved to the barn that was decorated with white material hanging down from the rafters and a chandelier that was tied to the middle rafter. There was only one long table, since our group wasn't large, placed near a big stone fireplace that was burning bright, heating up the space for us.

We jumped right into dancing our first song as husband and wife, thanks to the last-minute DJ doing what he does best.

The whole evening was filled with love, happiness, and laughter. The chaos in Seahill was forgotten for one night. Feelings of woe and helplessness were put on hold while everyone danced and enjoyed this moment with us.

"This is amazing. I love you so much." Rose wrapped her arms around me as we danced, much like that one time in Club V when we were staking out Emanuel. It seemed so long ago.

"Thank you for finding me and dragging me back into the light."

"You became our sun, Draco, like I said, but you're more than that to me. You're my sun, my moon, and all the stars in the universe. You are my world."

"And you are mine." I leaned in for a kiss, both of us smiling blissfully.

"I'm sorry, everyone, but we have to see this," Phillip announced to the room and turned on his phone, tapping something on it that made the screen project on the wall.

Dorian's face appeared in a room that looked much like the Oval Office.

"What is this?" I asked. Everyone's dancing stilled and watched the projected screen with complete attention.

"This is on every channel—he's at the capitol."

Dorian gave the camera an evil smirk, like we were all his toys and he was choosing who to play with first.

"Hello, world. It's time for you all to wake up. People with powers are among you, and we aren't going anywhere."

This was it—the darkness had finally come.

I looked at Rose and found her looking at me, both of us wishing we had more time to be happy in this moment together. But that peace was over.

It was time to get ready for war.

"The time has come for some changes to be made. There is no need for us to be hidden in the shadows; we are being set free. Fear us if you want, or you can join us. Either way, we are here. Tomorrow is the solar eclipse of the century. Darkness will cover the earth, and the age of the gifted will begin."

He leaned in closer, and I could feel he was staring at me directly.

"Heroes: try to stop us if you want, but you will lose everything if you do."

And just like that, he was gone, in a bright flash of light.

Chapter Thirty-Four

Dorian

I was dressed and ready to start implementing the next part of my plan.

The main set of my crew was waiting in the large training room, horsing around until it was their turn to be set free.

"Time to cause a little trouble. Ajax, you and Monica head to the bridge. Let's turn this island into a playground." I gave him the word, and he grinned. Monica walked over to me and touched her hands to my face. Just as she leaned in to try and kiss me, I turned my head.

"Get out of here," I gritted through my teeth and knocked her hand away from my skin.

She didn't look one bit regretful as she turned around and walked off with Ajax.

"Roady, do your thing and start the system shutdown. I want it all out." He got to work on his laptop, even though I knew he'd soon be moving to the large computer area I'd supplied him with.

Jesse was the host of Echo's gift. He had been able to shift into any animal at will after much practice, and with his strength, I knew any in his path would fall. He was sitting on the ground meditating, and hadn't looked at me since I walked in. That was fine, his time wasn't now.

Ajax and Monica would take out the bridge, and then the true chaos would start.

I flashed to a nearby rooftop to watch them work. It was very early in the morning, and the bridge was empty.

A large boom reverberated through the air, and piece by piece, the only way onto the island fell into the freezing water.

Phase two started immediately after the bridge fell. All the lights started to go out in the city, block by block. Electricity was no more.

You'd be surprised how much chaos can be caused just by cutting off people from electricity. The majority of mankind didn't know how to live without it—never had to fight to survive, or live off of the land like I had many years ago. It was time to take them back to those days.

The morning sun was just starting to crest over the mountain, and while police sirens and fire trucks were out in full force, and everyone trying to figure out what was happening, their efforts were futile.

Then I spotted it.

Light glaring in the sky from one section of the city.

I knew which one it was, and I had to give it up to them—I was impressed the kid had it in him.

AJ, the boy genius that Phillip had saved.

Roady and he would fight in the virtual world while the rest of us handled reality.

But for now, I would watch as humans destroyed themselves, as was their nature to do.

It wasn't long before the governor levied a mandatory curfew. Police were driving slowly around the streets, speaking to people through their radio speakers.

Of course, people didn't listen. They were in panic mode, which only intensified when word spread about the bridge being knocked out.

Looting, fighting, and fires were taking over.

I laughed. People loved to blame evil and bad deeds on the devil or some supernatural force, but really, it was all them. One little nudge and they did all the work themselves, damning them to whatever hell they were going to. I'd seen it all in my lifetime. Violence, greed...and when in pure desperation, they will do anything.

225

Kindness was harder to come by than the others, as everyone was so focused on themselves, unwilling to take the time to look up and be nice. To care for one another. Hell, I saw it plenty in the hospital. The elderly were dropped off and treated like old dogs who needed to be put down. The old became nuisances. Doctors being serial killers, and nurses being rapists and murderers. Or a doctor being the villain. Man didn't care about man, so there was no reason to protect them when the threat was really the person standing next to them.

Over the course of a few hours, cities all over the world were having battles of their own. The men and women I'd recruited were free, doing as they wished. Roady had done his job well, infecting the main systems of government with a virus that would take them at least two hours to break. It would be just enough time.

I stood on top of Griffin Enterprises, the tallest tower in Seahill, and watched as the moon started to cross into the path of the sun.

Chapter Thirty-Five

Draco

"I love you," I said as I pressed Rose hard against my chest, kissing her forehead.

We'd managed to stay together all morning, but she was needed somewhere else now. She was going to help Asher calm the city, although I feared it was impossible now. Dorian had created seeds of panic in people with his TV stunt. Now with the bridge out, and the electricity gone, people were in a state of feral terror.

She tilted her head and gave me a smile before leaning up to kiss me sweetly.

My hands gripped her soft green sweater, keeping her in my arms, where I could keep her safe. But she gave me a look.

"We need to help them. It's why we have these gifts—you showed us our true purpose, and we can't let them down. We can't let *you* down."

She always knew what to say. I hated her leaving me right now, but she was right.

"I'll see you soon," she said as she untangled herself from my arms and jogged off in Asher's direction.

Leon and Lilith were trying to find a way to get people off the island on some big hotshot's yacht. The day was only going to get worse, and the more casualties we could stop, the better.

Charles had once again been working with the police force in hopes that they could find the source of trouble and how to handle the riots in between.

AJ and Mina were battling the work of whoever Dorian had on his team, and last I heard they were getting ahead. The electrical grid of the city would be back up in half an hour.

Phillip had been helping the politicians, before they left via helicopter. Only the governor stayed behind to help evacuate people if we could secure the boats. He was an honorable man.

"It's all going to work." Phillip was pacing and then took off without another word to us.

"Come on. I've spotted Dorian at the top of Phillip's building." Echo had just changed from a hawk to human again, wrapping herself in a towel since there was no point in putting on real clothes when she'd turn right back into another animal soon.

"Phillip said we have to let him start whatever game he's playing with the sun, and allow him to bring about night. Then we attack. It's the only chance for righting this," I said, and while I could tell she was struggling with accepting my absolute trust in Phillip, she nodded then asked what we should do next.

"Let's get as many people as we can away from Griffin tower. I'm not sure talking will work, so scare tactics might be best. Got anything scary?" I asked, and she rolled her eyes.

"I'll do my best once we are there." She shifted shortly thereafter, morphing into a bear, and together we ran toward the largest tower in the city.

Leon showed up as soon as we got there and told us that they secured some boats to get off the island. Lilith was doing her best to keep everyone calm while loading them up.

"Everyone get to the harbor! You'll find a boat to get off the island!" I started yelling at every scared group of people I could. A police officer nearby noticed my words and started repeating them as well. Despite everything that had happened before, we were still heroes in the eyes of some people. We'd stood our ground and were here to help when shit hit the fan.

"Leon, go pull all the fire alarms, get people away from this tower and out of it," I directed, and he was off in a blur to do as told. The bells started ringing and shortly thereafter people came pouring out. I was glad to see that a lot of people had already left the island before today, fleeing inland after Dorian's warning on TV. The people who'd been rioting and looting had also disappeared from this area. I hoped that they'd heard about getting to the water, where they'd at least make it to physical safety. Their actions would probably cause mental anguish, but that was treatable if they lived.

I looked at the bear to my right that was doing a great job at scaring people to the harbor. She saw my look and changed into a large python. Several people saw the snake and began screaming hysterically and running for the water.

Well, it was cruel, but it would get the job done.

Echo slithered around, and everyone ran for their lives. Gone was the threat of the world ending—all they cared about was escaping the giant snake.

I don't really know how we did it, to be honest, but an hour later a majority of the people had been evacuated off the island successfully. Anyone who had stayed behind was accepting the fate that came to them or wanted to fight beside us.

There were only a few of those: one with powers that controlled water, although he wasn't trained to use it since he'd hidden his secret for years, and four regular humans with no extra gifts.

I admired their spirit, and while normally I would deny their help, I couldn't get the words out that they were in over their heads. They deserved to fight for their lives as much as we did.

"Oh, hell," someone cursed, and I looked over to see the water controller looking up.

"Don't look at it, you'll go blind!" I yelled and headed for the doors to the tower.

"Whatever you do, keep this tower secure. Dorian's crew is around, and I have a feeling they'll come to him once darkness takes over," I said, looking each person in the face.

I could have stopped this, many years ago, but I'd been blind.

Dorian had been there all along, I should have seen it. I should have looked for him. I shouldn't have stopped trying to make things right.

I'd damned them all.

One step in front of the other, I walked into the glass building, and made my way up the twenty flights of stairs toward my brother, and my enemy.

Chapter Thirty-Six

Dorian

My body glowed with the power of the sun's radiation, absorbing every ray I could get.

I took it all, sunlight from all around the globe coming to me like a blast of light. Soon nothing but darkness would cover the earth. It would only last one solid day, but that was enough. I wasn't asshole enough to doom the planet by holding the light within me until the plants wilted and nature slowly died. But I wanted suffering like my people had suffered. Like I suffered. So, keeping them alive was a necessity to that.

The moon had completely covered the sun, and now the night would take over.

When the last bit of sunlight was absorbed into my veins, my vision became tinged with a glow, and a subtle current ran over my skin. *So much power.*

"Dorian."

As I knew he would, Draco had showed up a few seconds too late.

"Congrats on evacuating the city. Now we can destroy it without simpletons getting in the way." I shrugged. My voice was deeper than before, the power inside me making everything I was more charged. My father had once told me that he felt like he was always harboring light, like a vessel, and it was a constant battle to keep the light contained during the night. I could understand his struggle.

I turned to see Draco standing by the rooftop's only entrance and exit door. He ran up here and barely looked out of breath. Impressive.

"I beseech you, brother, it's not too late. All isn't lost—we can still be the light in the darkness together."

He was seriously trying again to bring me over to the side of the heroes.

"I am the light *and* the darkness. It's too late, brother." I spit out the last word. He wasn't my brother, and though we shared the blood of Apollo together, he was nothing but an enemy to me.

"Then there is no good inside you." He knew that, but had tried to find some humanity in me anyway.

"I am the villain in this story—have been for over a millennium."

I could see the future in my head spin to what he was going to say next, and I cut him off instead.

"No use in using her in your cause; you'll only piss me off further."

She was not part of this fight, and I would keep her name out of it for as long as I could.

"Then it comes down to us," he sighed. Our battle was about to begin.

"It was always about us. This whole story has always been down to us—everyone else was just a side character. Easily disposable. Now, I have a world to take over, so let's move this along. I've seen the ending enough times to know that you fail against my sword and lose those you care about. I'm quite eager to see that defeated look on your face in the present." I positioned myself for the lunge that was coming, and even when his arms went around my waist, throwing us off the side of the tallest building in the city, I was prepared.

I flashed us to another building, and his fist came swinging toward my face as soon as our feet touched the ground. Dodging him was easier this time. I had a cleared head and could focus on his movements instead of Esme's like before.

We traded blows, and I flashed to another building.

My hand moved up and pressed against his shoulder, pushing the light out through my hand. Draco flew back with a nasty burn on his skin. Sunlight was quite potent, especially in concentrated doses like that.

He rose and came back at me, even with his charred skin exposed to the cold.

"Things are getting too predictable, Draco, I think we need to shake this scene up a bit." I moved to the side of his punch and touched his shoulder, digging my fingers into his wound and flashing us to where the heroes were surrounding Griffin tower. My crew was just coming out of the shadows.

I dropped Draco in front of his woman, who glared at me with hatred in her eyes as she helped Draco to his feet.

Her powers were caressing my brain, wanting me to open up to her and let those emotions wash over me. To control me.

"I'm immune, darling." I winked at her and looked around the nearly empty city, the only inhabitants the few who stupidly thought to stand their ground against me.

"Your Hero Society is over. Join me and be free. Live the life you want without fear, or persecution from humans, who just days before this were willing to hurt you. They abandoned you, and yet you stand here for them? Give up the righteous cause! The gods were fools, and they died because the humans gave up on them. Don't follow their fate."

I did try, although I knew none of them would waiver. Good versus evil. To them there was no in-between. But life didn't work that way—there was a middle ground. Good people could do bad things for good reasons, and vice versa.

No one spoke, as I expected.

"You guys want a fight?" I looked at Phillip and waited for the puppet master to make his move. We'd both been playing the same game, and both of us had chosen a path to follow. The outcomes were dwindling as we stood here staring at each other.

Seeing all the heroes here at once made my blood boil. Maybe I was a sucker for pain, but I wanted the fight right now.

The more I looked at them, the more I saw her face, and the more I wanted pain. The desire to destroy everything that made her pop into my head was overwhelming.

They all looked at me with a mixture of hate and pity in their eyes.

"Let's dance, heroes."

And just like that, the city was a battle ground, and only one side could win.

Everyone matched up with someone they figured were their equal in a fight: Leon and Ajax, Lilith and Monica, Phillip and Ron Presley, the kid from the hospital who could read minds.

Jesse and Echo had taken forms of animals and were battling like ones. Asher had caught the eye of Trix, a magician whose power was over shadows. He could become them and manipulate them. I wished I had time to watch that fight, but Draco was coming my way. He and I were the only true warriors in this battle. He was mine to finish.

Rose was fighting with a newcomer of their team that could play with water and the humans who stayed.

The rest of my army would handle them.

Chapter Thirty-Seven

Draco

I heard the battle cries, the grunting, and shrieks of pain.

It didn't have to be like this.

People were going to die, and I didn't know how to stop it. I pleaded with Dorian, and now the only option I see to end this is to end him. Cut off the head of the snake. The body will wiggle around for a bit, but then it will die.

We fought, both of us taking hits, blood coating our teeth from punches to the face.

Sometimes he would let me land a painful blow, as if he wanted it. Not once did he touch his sword to fight me, even though it was there, ready and waiting to slice me. As if he liked the pain of my fists.

I couldn't die, and while I would grow weary, the energy would come back to me quickly. He was still riding on sunlight, which would last him for days or until he gave it back to earth.

This Dorian was different than our last fight, when he almost died. He was focused and lethal, moving faster, anticipating moves either from watching me or seeing the future in his head. We could keep this going for days.

I looked around for something that could help me.

"You wanna make things more interesting?" He took a step back and flashed away. Moments later he was back and throwing a sword at me, aiming straight for my chest. I moved quickly out of the trajectory and then caught it as it tried to go past me.

"So fast," he mocked and then reached above his head, wrapping his fingers slowly around the hilt, pulling his sword up and back around to his front.

Swords.

A true warrior's weapon.

We would fight like ancient Greeks until the death, it seemed. Although it was obvious Dorian had trained after our original ancient time, I'd been brought up to fight since I could stand.

This was a battle he would not win.

I didn't say a word as I raised my sword into position, taking deep breaths to calm and focus my mind. But then I heard a female cry out in agony, follow by a bellow of rage.

I wanted to look, to make sure it wasn't one of my own, but Dorian took my momentary loss of attention and attacked first.

I vaguely heard Rose's cry of sadness, but I knew she was alive. She was strong, but one of ours was hurt.

His sword clashed with mine, hard and loud.

He was done letting me get in free hits so he could feel the pain. This moment with steel was personal, and his rage was fueling him. He was all precision and skill as he was on the offense.

The whole area had become a war zone, and as we moved around the street, I saw the others in my peripheral vision, and my heart stopped.

Leon and Lilith were in the grass, lying together in each other's arms, dead.

Pure, undiluted anger poured into my veins.

Dorian saw them and smirked. That smirk would be his undoing.

He came at me, and I pushed him back, moving quickly on my feet at the attacker now. He dodged and blocked my attacks, and while he had

241

many years of practice and skill, I had years of experience.

Feeling like an asshole, I taunted him with my technique.

Pieces of building fell around us, and we were forced to separate or be crushed under the rubble. I had taken a moment to glance at my comrades when I saw movement coming. I didn't care about Dorian, or anything else, as I took off into a sprint. All that mattered was stopping what I knew would be the end.

But I wasn't fast enough.

My arms wrapped around her soft body, falling to the ground.

My Rose...my wife.

Her eyes were wide as they stared at my face.

"I'm sorry." Tears flowed over my cheeks as the feeling of helplessness settled over me. There was nothing I could do. I looked down at the knife plunged into her stomach and began to weep harder.

"I love you." My eyes moved back to her face, and I saw her looking at me with tears flooding her gaze. We both knew she was dying, that there was no fixing this wound.

"It wasn't enough time." I shook my head. We knew one day I would outlive her, but this? I thought we would have more time. I needed more time. I'd prayed for many years for time to end and take me with it, but now all I could think of was my need for more.

"Be with me till our time runs out." Her hand was trying to reach mine, but she was weak. Instantly I wrapped my free hand around hers. Opening myself up to her, I felt her fears, her sadness, and her love.

"I'll always be with you, no matter how long you live, old man." She tried to smile but a cough shook her, blood tinging the edges of her mouth.

"My love..." I was breaking with every shallow breath she took.

I'd seen this future before it came to be, that losing her would be the end of me. I'd never recover.

She didn't speak but pushed the entirety of her love into me until it filled me, drawing a sob from my chest.

"I promise I'll find a way to you, my wife," I vowed.

"I love you so—" She tried to say more, but her body was giving up. I held her hand, feeling everything she felt, when suddenly all emotions were gone.

My wife was dead.

Chapter Thirty-Eight

Dorian

Death permeated the air around us.

Loss was inevitable on both sides, and both sides were prepared to die when they chose to fight.

Everyone had stopped fighting while Draco held his dying love on the ground.

My chest hurt, seeing them.

Seeing the great General Draco in tears as the woman he loved took her final breath.

The memory of me holding Esme's dying body in my arms, watching the light leave her eyes, flooded my brain. Every soft curve of her body in that blue dress, the way her lips parted from being too weak, her hazel eyes filled with love as she looked at me.

Rose and Draco had looked at each other with love until she died.

I'd only stared at Esme in shock for what she'd done.

Echo, still in wolf form, began to howl for the loss of her friend, bringing my attention to the present. Phillip was crying and running his fingers through his hair. He gambled wrong with all of their lives, and now he'd have to live with the death of his sister. He could have stopped it; he could have stopped all of this, but he didn't.

The fighting around us began again once Echo attacked the man who'd stabbed Rose, crushing his neck with one bite as she shook her head like the man was a rag doll between her teeth.

I stared at the back of Draco, still holding his dead woman.

"You and I weren't made to love." I took a step closer, watching as he slowly pulled the knife out of her gut, placing her hands gently across the wound before lowering her to the ground.

"Goodbye, my wife." He stood, keeping his eyes on her.

I'd known a future of them marrying was probable, though for them, what was the point? He would outlive her no matter what.

He grabbed hold of the sword that he'd thrown to the ground and turned to face me.

I knew the expression on his face. I knew it because I saw that expression on my own after Esme died.

But I didn't love her.

He didn't speak as he approached me, sword at his side. Then he stopped, tears on his cheeks.

"I'd live and suffer for a thousand more years if I got to feel her love for me, even for one minute. I cherished her, I loved her, and I wouldn't change a damn thing. She was my everything. You had love, and you threw it away like garbage; you are the one who truly suffers between us."

His sword rose and moved to strike.

Renewed focus to end me was lit inside him.

He fought harder—faster—and I knew he wanted us both to leave this earth tonight.

But that focus in his head was diminished, and the agony of loss took over. It was easy, the movement that impaled my sword into his chest, almost as if he wanted me to do it, but he wouldn't die despite how much he wished it.

My mind was racing, trying to catch up with all the feelings inside me. This wasn't how I expected I'd feel. Something wasn't right.

I looked into the future, seeing it as clear as I had before.

Phillip was walking toward me.

"You've lost, and we are free," I stated, instead of the battle cry I'd seen in my future as Draco fell, sword to his chest.

He would heal, of course, but he would never truly live now that his love was gone.

Those who remained of the army on my side raised their fists in victory.

"We won't ever give up. Remember that, Dorian," Echo called out. She was completely bare, her body covered in dirt and blood after having fought in her animal's forms. Asher was by her side, but there was blood rushing down his head. He would survive; I'd seen it. So would she.

They looked down at their fallen comrades. Phillip's sister was lying on the ground, eyes closed, hands resting on her bleeding stomach, where Draco had placed them gently after she died.

Leon and Lilith were embraced together on the grass. She had sacrificed herself to save his good soul from going to hell, damning them both to perish together. At least they had that.

Everything was playing out as the future had shown me, but something didn't feel right. Something was wrong, and I couldn't figure it out.

Phillip rushed to Draco's side and pulled out the sword in one quick motion, blood pouring out from his wound. When I'd seen this in my vision, I had hoped it would hurt. Watching it now only made a grimace grace my lips.

Still, I tried to continue the course I'd chosen.

"You chose wrong, Griffin, and you lost everything." I stared at him, speaking with no venom in my words like I should have had.

"You never deserved the love she gave you," Phillip said, but he didn't lunge at me like he had in my vision.

"What did you do?" I was at a complete loss. I was aching inside my body, not in the physical way but deeper, in my soul, if I had one.

Phillip stood and faced me.

"You're realizing you loved Esme."

I shook my head. No, I wasn't. Esme and I had a short moment together, a passing star in the night sky. Bright and beautiful, but was over quickly.

"You loved her and lost her, as Draco has lost my sister. She died in your arms, though you pushed it far back into your mind until seeing them together. Hearing Rose take her last breath brought out those repressed feelings. You're feeling Esme's love, and you're feeling the loss of that love." Phillip was standing his ground.

"I didn't love her!" I roared.

But even I felt it was a lie now. I'd found love where it wasn't supposed to be, it was right in front of me the whole time.

"It doesn't matter. There's nothing we can do now. Let's be done." I tried hard to push back the feelings of regret and sorrow that were trying to consume me.

"It's not done, Dorian. We can change it. We can change it all. Bring them all back." I looked at him like he'd lost his mind. Losing his sister had made him go mad. His words were impossible.

Even the gods hadn't liked to play with bringing people back from the dead. It never ended well.

"Give it up, Griffin. Mourn your dead and be free." I started to walk away when his next words stopped me.

"You could have a second chance with her. To love her." His eyes were pleading me to take a leap on whatever he was trying to sell me.

I couldn't help myself as I tilted my head and looked up at the stars that were peeking through the false night sky.

She would see me as a monster if she was here. But would she still love me? If it were possible to change things, would she still love me after all I've done? I didn't think so.

I kept walking, my heart hurting with the knowledge that I was choosing for things to stay as they were in fear that she'd no longer love the villain who'd killed her friends and took away the light, despite my revelation of my own love.

"Stop running away from your feelings! Help me change the Fates' design, Dorian. Help me bring them back!" I kept moving.

"Why do you fight it? Why won't you give in?" he yelled while stomping after me. I'd had enough.

"Because I love her!" I yelled.

"I loved her, and I don't wanna see that look in her eyes now that it's too late."

Movement from behind Phillip caught my eye. Draco was healed and moving toward us. His eyes weren't filled with hate—instead they beamed with hope. He would move mountains to be with Rose again; he would do anything to hold her in his arms.

I felt shame for the first time in so long.

What was I willing to do to have Esme again?

Chapter Thirty-Nine

Draco

I saw the war in his eyes: the pain, the hope, and the fear.

"We have to make it right. For them. I don't care what I have to do, I'm willing to give her better than this." I looked to my love who lay on the cold ground.

Phillip and I both watched Dorian as he sorted through his mind.

"It's not possible." He deflated, and I knew he felt as I did. Love had finally wrapped itself around his heart, driving him to make things right. For Esme.

"Between you two, we have the blood of the actual gods of ancient Greece. All we need is a little magic." Phillip looked down to Asher, who was holding Echo in his arms.

The few that were left in Dorian's crew had left when they saw the war raging inside him, the turning of change stirring in the air.

"It's going to take a lot of power what you're asking of me." Asher's eyebrows narrowed but he kissed Echo's head before giving her his torn leather jacket to cover her up and headed toward us.

Dorian and I both exchanged confused glances.

"We have the power of the gods right here. Can't get any more powerful than that."

"Explain," I asked, since there seemed to be something I wasn't aware of.

"Asher is spotty in all the visions of future. I can sometimes see him, but sometimes I can't. He and I had an in-depth conversation weeks ago about his people, and magic. I believe we can turn back time with his help. It's hard, but not impossible. You both have the gods inside you, unlike us, that just host their powers. Your blood and Asher's magic can go back to before this began. Before Rose wound up in your coop, or before Esme and you got together. Before this whole war."

Phillip spoke with complete confidence, but there was more to this whole situation—I could feel it.

"What's the catch?" Dorian asked first, voicing what I was thinking.

"Draco becomes mortal, and everyone we bring back might not remember any of this. All these months could be gone from their mind."

My whole body froze hearing his words.

Mortal.

Rose might not remember me, her husband.

I shook myself out of it and answered quickly.

"Let's do it."

Immortality was nothing without her, and if there was a chance she wouldn't remember me, I'd be there to remind her that she is mine. She would remember me, though. I had faith in love. Love was going to be what saved us all, including Dorian.

Dorian looked angry but nodded.

"This isn't going to be pleasant—in fact, it's going to feel like fire in your blood and your muscles are being pulled from your bones," Asher said flatly and walked over to Dorian's sword that was lying on the ground where Phillip had tossed it after pulling it from my chest.

"Or at least that's what the legends say it feels like. Could be worse."

Asher was in no mood for joking. Couldn't say I blamed him. Our family was broken, and we were joining sides with the man who caused it all, to bring them back.

But I knew the heartache that Dorian was suffering from. He'd kept Esme's death inside, unwilling to accept what he felt. Seeing my pain and Rose die in my arms brought it all out for him as if it was happening in the present.

"See you in the past," Phillip said as he took steps back to stand next to Echo, wrapping his hand in hers. I could see them both sending us prayers of hope that this would work, that we could right our wrongs, both Dorian and me.

"Fuck, I'm glad we are going back because I would probably be murdered by my old coven for doing this." Asher looked at the sword and cursed.

Dorian looked at me, and I saw he would do whatever it took to have Esme back, his hatred for me and whatever bitterness he had held on to for so long was nothing compared to his love for her.

Love had saved us all.

"I call upon the elements of time and space."

Asher closed his eyes and raised the sword in the air.

"Lend me your energy for all of the human race. I invoke the sun, the stars, and the moon—the keepers of time."

Wind picked up around us, spinning around as if a tornado was brewing and we were right in the eye. His magic was doing something, that was for sure.

"Fire and sky will fall for the sacrifice."

Thunder shuddered through the sky, and lightning shot down in a burst of light and electricity right to the sword, as if the metal was absorbing the firebolt.

"Holy fuck." Dorian was stunned, as was I, having never seen anything like that in all my years.

"Give me your hands," Asher demanded, and we moved to follow his command.

He gripped my hand first, shoving that sword that seemed to be made of lightning into my hand, slicing my skin. It burned like hell, and I felt electricity travel through my blood to every part of me.

He moved to Dorian quickly, doing the same.

We both hissed as the pain began to intensify.

"Blood of man, blood of a god, and blood of the immortal."

He brought that sword to his hand and sliced his own. Our blood ran from our hands to the ground, where each droplet burst into flames like drops of fire falling from the sky.

The wind picked up around us further. Phillip and Echo had to move farther away or be caught in the storm that was brewing.

"Bend the powers that be, unnatural energy, I invoke thee."

Lightning was dropping from the sky all around us, shattering concrete, towers, and whatever else it could connect with.

"I don't think your magic likes this very much," Dorian commented, and Asher shot him a look that said his statement was obvious.

"Keepers of time and space, a line of the past I trace. We bend thee, we bend thee, we bend thee." The sword of lightning started to glow before he seemed to struggle, moving it over him, then with all the might he could muster, he drove it into the ground where our blood had mingled together. My body exploded into excruciating pain.

Chapter Forty

Dorian

I'd been tortured before. I'd been stabbed through the chest with rebar.

The pain that was overtaking my body, as well as Asher and Draco's, was indescribable.

It was like being thrown into lava while high-voltage electricity was hooked straight to your veins.

We'd all fallen to our knees before the sword that was streaming a bright light to the sky above.

I could barely keep my eyes open to see that the world around us was beginning to shift.

"I have to pull the sword at the right moment." Asher gritted out his words before his head flew back from a surge of torment that blasted through this break in time.

We tried to focus on what was happening, but the pain was trying to claim us.

"Almost there." Asher tried to stand but was pushed to the ground again. The powers we were fucking with were unnatural, but here we were.

He rose to his hands and knees, trying to crawl to the sword.

"Fuck this." I pushed against the gravity that was trying to flatten me against the earth while I suffered.

A bellow of pain erupted from my chest as lightning hit me, and when it left my body, all the power from the sun and light I'd taken earlier was ripped from my body.

Digging my fingers into the ground, I moved slow, but I managed to wrap my hands around Asher and push him forward, using my strength to get him to the sword. Draco had joined me as we used our bodies to move the witch.

He cried out in pain, gripping the hilt with everything he had and pulling, chanting something I couldn't focus on because of the agony inside my own body wreaking havoc.

Then it was over.

We were thrown back as the world stopped spinning from the force. Everything still hurt, but nothing like before. It was more of a soreness you'd get from being in a car accident.

"Good job, guys. You did it."

Phillip's voice penetrated the air, and I sat up to look around. Everything was back to normal. The sky was blue with the sun shining, and people were walking around like they hadn't been part of a supernatural war. Phillip was standing there in clean clothes, looking more chipper than ever.

Draco tried to talk but couldn't get the words out. I tried, and nothing. My throat was dry and felt like it was burned.

"It'll come back soon. Everyone is alive and kicking. I can tell you where they are, but we have to talk first."

We all were starting to stand on shaky legs, while Phillip narrowed his sight on me.

"We have a chance to start over, to do things the proper way, and learn from our mistakes. You gave up your hate for love. I trust you have no plans on going back to your villainous ways?"

I could see both Draco and Asher tensing, ready to fight me again, depending on my answer.

"It's done."

Might as well embrace this new path of mortality and be...happy for once.

"No more immortality?" He went further, and I shook my head. I'd give that up too. Immortality was a pain in the ass, and after having felt things I never wanted to feel again, I didn't want to outlive Esme.

Esme. I ached to go and see her. Would she remember us together? Or still see me as the asshole doctor I was before?

"Great. Welcome to Seahill, one year prior to when you left the city in chaos. People without gifts don't remember a thing. The rest of us, it just depends. Some do, and some don't. There is not another you in this time. You and your body before merged. Complicated stuff, but just know you won't be running into a you from one year ago. I suggest you go on with the life you had, and we will figure out how to make the Hero Society better than it ever was before. Yes, Dorian, I am including you in this. You're welcome to join our little club." Phillip smirked, and I rolled my eyes. That invitation would be sitting on the table for a while.

"Okay. Now, about your loves: Rose is at her apartment. Esme is at the hospital working, and Echo is driving to her apartment. We got second chances, guys, let's not fuck it up."

I didn't waste time, and neither did the others. I flashed to my office, which looked the same as I remembered it a year ago. Not even bothering to change out of my clothes, I opened the door and went looking for Esme.

I looked into the future and saw the many possibilities. Ones where she didn't remember me, ones where she did, ones where she hated me, and ones where she forgave me.

It was a leap of faith trying to find her, but I was already past the point of no return. I went back in time and let go of my hate, for her. I would at least try.

I racked my brain to remember what part of the hospital she was in a year ago, but that was back when I was an asshole who thought she was a waste of time.

Complete asshole.

I spotted Melissa Ann at the nurses' station. Her eyes wide, taking in my appearance. Dried blood from the slices Draco had made—thankfully the golden tint had faded a while ago, so no one would see that. My clothes looked like shit, and I knew it must have blown her mind.

"Dr. Dorian, were you in an accident? We should get those wounds of yours checked out immediately." She rushed around the desk and tried to start checking me over.

I shrugged her off easily.

"I'm fine. Where is Esme?" I asked, and Melissa shook her head.

"I'll get her for you, if you agree to be looked at." She crossed her arms over her chest and stood tall. The woman was being ridiculous. Still, the advantage was Esme would come to me instead of me barreling into her by surprise.

"Fine." She ushered me into a room and took my vitals; they were fine, as I knew they would be. My wounds would need to be cleaned, and for some, stitches were required.

"I want Esme to do them," I stated, and Melissa sighed.

"Be nice to her today. She's been in a sad mood, and I don't want you making it worse," she said right before she left the room.

I didn't say anything. Now that I was paying attention to everyone's reaction about Esme and me, instead of getting annoyed like I was before, I wanted to prove them wrong. Show everyone, including her, that I was the man she deserved.

A small knock on the door brought my attention to the present, and my breath got stuck in my chest.

The door handle moved, and the door opened slowly.

"Dr. Dorian, what shit have you gotten yourself into today?" Esme entered the room, and I completely forgot how to breathe, my eyes glued to the beautiful woman who was staring at me with hazel eyes filled with annoyance.

Chapter Forty-One

Esme

Dorian was wide-eyed as he looked over me, in shock at seeing me alive.

I had to admit seeing the look on his face made me feel hope that something crucial had changed in him. I know something big had happened in the world since I was alive, even though I remember dying.

Still, I didn't know what happened, and while I was beyond happy to see him, I wanted to know where we stood. Was this the Dorian that was an asshole to me, or the one that despite everything made me fall for him?

"Esme." His voice was barely above a whisper, and I felt that hope inside me flutter.

My fingers reached out to touch his wounds, and his body shuddered against my touch. A good shudder or a bad one?

"Did you get in a fight with a knife while dicing vegetables?" I teased, a defense for the strong feelings that were running through me right now.

"No, Esme. How are you feeling? Melissa Ann said you were sad today."

"Today has been a weird one, that's for sure, but if I'm being honest, I do feel sad."

"Why?"

He was just as unsure in this moment as I was.

Something had changed in him. I could see it in his eyes, his wariness being around me.

Dare I keep hoping he realized his feelings for me? Instead of ruining the world, he somehow saved it and brought me back?

"Well, it's sort of a long story. I don't want to bother you with my feelings. I know how much you detest emotions."

I couldn't get my words out, for some reason, even though I saw that something was different, I was still guarding my heart.

"Maybe this would help you loosen your tongue." He stood, closing the small distance in between us. My eyes drifted up to his, my heart beating faster in my chest.

"I love you, Esme. Sorry I was too big of an asshole to see it."

As cliché as it was, my legs gave out, but Dorian was quick to wrap his arms around me while sitting back in the chair and bringing me with him onto his lap.

"I hope those are tears of happiness." He spoke softly while reaching up to wipe the tears that were falling down my cheeks.

"The man I sacrificed my life for loves me back. Of course they are happy tears, you jerk."

I was being overly emotional, but considering I'd died for him, and then was suddenly back in a place where he loved me, I think my happy tears were acceptable.

"You remember everything?" he asked, as if still scared that I might not, and I nodded my head.

"I remember everything. What did you do, Dorian? Why do you look like you were in an explosion?" My hands started running all over his skin, touching every part of him I could, making sure he was real.

"Are you sure you want to hear it?"

"Yes." I knew without a doubt I wanted to know.

"I started a war, and people died, but seeing one particular person take their last breath opened my eyes. And love won. Asher was able to work a spell with my and Draco's blood to go back in time. A time where you were living. I gave it all up to see you breathing again and to tell you I love you."

My smile was wide, and my tears wouldn't stop flowing.

"Do you hate me?" His hand left my side and cupped my cheek. He made mistakes, big ones, but in the end, he made it better.

"I knew falling for the villain wouldn't be easy, but turns out the villain was really the hero in the end." I couldn't help the laugh that bubbled from my chest as a big smile grew on his face before he leaned in and pressed his lips against mine.

"I love you, Dorian," I mumbled against him before the kiss deepened. We gained back the time that was lost to us, and we weren't giving up one minute of right now without touching.

We kissed for what seemed like eternity before a knock made our lips break apart. Melissa Ann bustled into the room.

"I'm fully expecting to be your matron of honor since I called this from the beginning." She stood there with her arms over her chest and a big-ass grin on her lips.

Dorian laughed, and I couldn't help but join in.

"Well, if you two are done cannoodling, we need to patch Dorian up and clean this room. I've covered for you, Esme, and afterward you two can head out."

I didn't need to say it, because she saw the words expressed on my face. Melissa Ann was the bomb.

In no time, Dorian's wounds were cleaned and he was stitched up. He promised that he would go into more detail about it later, but as soon as we left the hospital together he flashed us to his stunning apartment by the bay. He needed a wash and a change of clothes, so of course it was natural that I helped him get clean in the shower.

For hours we talked, we cherished each other's bodies, and we loved hard.

A whole new world of possibilities had opened up to us. But the first thing I wanted to do when we came out of the apartment was to head to the Hero Society.

They'd become my family, and I had to see what happened to them, make sure they were okay.

"You don't have to come if you don't want to."

Separating my life with them and with him would be difficult. But Dorian didn't stop walking as we moved closer to headquarters.

Chapter Forty- Two

Esme

The restaurant was under construction. I'd forgotten that headquarters had been very new.

We walked around to the back parking lot and saw everyone there, all smiles, and embraces as we neared them.

A few people smiled when they saw me, but their smiles faded quickly when they spotted the man next to me.

Only Phillip, Draco, and Asher were unmoving.

"So, I guess I'm not the only one back from the dead." I tried to break the tension between us all, and it worked. Laughs erupted and then I was swarmed by the ladies of the society.

"Why is he here?" Leon asked in a confused voice.

"I go where Esme goes," Dorian replied confidently.

Phillip stepped up to the plate and decided to enlighten us all about what had happened, and where we'd go from there.

"Asher, with the help of Dorian and Draco, broke into time and reversed it to a place where everyone was alive, and the trouble hadn't begun. I'm pleased everyone has their memories, and I hope you'll find it in your hero hearts to forgive Dorian. I've invited him to join us if he wishes, to be a part of our family. He's let go of his villainous ways and became the hero that saved us all. As for what we do now...we have a second chance. We start fresh, learn from our mistakes, and be the heroes to mankind we were originally meant to be."

That was something I could get behind. My eyes roamed over everyone and saw they were in agreement too. We had something not many people got—a do-over. We had to make the best out of this rare opportunity.

Draco pulled Rose into his arms, squeezing her tightly, and Lilith looked at them with her wide smile while Leon snuggled her in as well.

Dorian wrapped his hand in mine, and we stood there as the sun rose, a new dawn for a new day.

"To a new start, and to the new adventures that await us all." I raised our combined hands in a toast.

"Come on, Rose, you know it's your turn to do your thing." Lilith bit her lip, and everyone laughed.

"You guys are nuts." Rose blushed and tried to hide her face but that wasn't happening.

"Give your fans what they want, beautiful," Draco teased, and she shook her head. Slowly Rose stood taller in the arms of her love, looking at every one of us with those strong eyes.

"We are heroes in the darkest times, and we will always rise to fight the shadows of the world of mankind. It's what we do."

Everyone hooted and cheered, and she shook her head with a chuckle. Dorian just rolled his eyes, but his grip tightened for a minute around my hand.

We would make him one of us soon enough.

Epilogue

Phillip

I watched my hero family hug and smile at being reunited. All of their futures flashed into my head, and I knew that all the pain, and all the suffering, was worth it in the end. I'd seen the brightest future and followed that path to a T.

Draco and Rose got married again; this time their wedding was on his property that had been destroyed before. The cows mooed and the chickens clucked as their caretakers said I do.

Rose became a guidance counselor at the local high school in hopes that future generations of sixteen-year-olds that came into their powers would have someone to talk to, to know that they weren't alone.

Draco continued his work training heroes to use their powers and teaching about the gods and their sacrifices, in hope of protecting mankind.

But perhaps my favorite future to look at, as I stared at my sister while she gazed into Draco's eyes, was the one I'd seen all along and fought for.

Draco's hair had been dusted with gray as he chased his youngest son around the yard while Rose pushed their one daughter and middle son on the swing set I'd bought them for Christmas. They laughed and smiled big, living a beautiful life together. In the end, they knew they'd continue to grow old and would die in one another's arms.

My eyes moved to the crazy couple and enjoyed peeking into their future too.

Lilith and Leon were on his sailboat, enjoying a proper honeymoon on the sea.

Happy his friend Charles accepted him again and had been healed by Dorian and Asher together, he was free of his guilt and could give himself fully to his wife.

Leon and Lilith became the mighty duo of the Hero Society. Lilith was a role model to many little girls of the world—that you could be pretty, wild, and strong. Leon started up a football team for people with powers, and together they worked toward making people feel accepted for being different.

Leon and Lilith loved their one little girl and traveled the world as a family, with Seahill as their home base.

Echo's laugh broke into my thoughts, and I quickly looked at them to see Asher being a goof to make his woman smile, as always.

Echo stayed on with the police department, which allowed her to help protect and serve as a hero with both her powers and with a badge. Asher continued to run his bar, which became a hot spot for people with powers to hang out and feel comfortable.

Together they had four beautiful children and had a small wedding, mending the bridge with his coven since he'd married into a strong line and provided even stronger heirs.

They were often out in the woods, holding hands, and enjoying nature as a family. The couple were truly mates in every sense of the word. It had given us hope that people who were unalike in power and magic could love. Humans and those with gifts could accept each other.

Lastly, my gaze fell on Esme and Dorian. I wasn't lying to her when I said her love was the making of legends.

Dorian continued his work at the hospital with Esme while they both helped the Hero Society when they could.

Esme had kept faith in her love for Dorian, and it saved the world. He loved her, and he spent every day after she was brought back proving it to her. He was still open to causing mischief here and there, surprisingly with the other males of the society at his side. But what transpired between Esme and Dorian was written in books. Stories were told of love conquering over all.

Dorian had taken care of the people who remembered him before and were waiting on a war that would never come. He apologized and helped them to see the error of their thinking.

He donated his other properties to house and train future heroes, since the headquarters under the restaurant had become too small for our growing society.

Esme gave birth to twins, both of the new parents in tears as they never thought they'd experience having children.

They grew old, having lived strong and loved hard.

Movement caught my eye as two forms were walking over to us. My heart picked up as I saw AJ and Mina. She was wearing her bored expression until she saw me. Being human, neither her nor AJ remembered the months that we'd lost when going back into time. But AJ had been with me before, and he would be on my side until the end.

I'd told him where to find his sister, knowing she'd want to meet me, the man that united them.

Mina was asleep on the couch with our daughter in her arms, both of them wearing matching unicorn onesies after waiting up for me while I was out trying to save a building full of people in a fire.

We'd had a large wedding, because Mina was my queen and deserved whatever she wanted. We were a match in every way, and even though I knew all the futures that could happen, she still found ways to surprise me. I'd seen her for many years before I'd gotten to look at her in real life, and she still took my breath away, all spunk and fire.

My girls. The reason I'd fought so hard and suffered. For this moment.

Without a word exchanged between us, Mina jumped at me and hugged my body tightly. I caught her, knowing it was coming, and while I knew it was only because she had her brother back, I hugged her in return, knowing that I would make her fall in love with me again, and our daughter's arrival wouldn't be far behind.

THE END

Or is it?

For those heroes, it is.

But there is always someone in need of protecting, and the Hero Society will be there to save them.

A spin-off is coming.

More Books by Jessica Florence

The Final KO

I fight bitches for a living.

Which makes finding a decent guy hard when you're a female MMA fighter. None of them have been my equal. I yearn for a man who can push me to reach new heights and challenge me. A man who will treat me like a lady then lift me up by my ass and impale me against the wall.

But when Arson Kade, MMA's top fighter and notorious manwhore, declares he's that man for me I have my doubts. Any sane woman would.

There seems to be more to Arson than the rumors that surround him, but will it make me fall hard or run for the hills?
I know I've got no choice but to hold on for the ride.

It's the main event and my heart's on the line.
But will it be the Final KO?

The Final Chase

I never thought a wallaby, Henley shirts, and a
horse's rectal exam would have anything in
common.
Turns out they did.
Jake Wild. Owner of Wild Rescue for exotic
animals.
He's everything I'm not, my polar opposite.
I'm heels and my salon,
he's dirt and his creatures.
But much like the animals he cares for, he's got
that carnal edge.
He's the type of man you crawl on your hands
and knees for with your ass up in the air.
He bites, he's on the hunt, and now I'm his prey.
A chance meeting and a bet started the
undeniable attraction between us.
But I'm not giving my heart and soul away that
easy, he's going to have to catch me first.
It's the ultimate game of cat and mouse.
But will it be the Final Chase?

Long Drive

There is a long road in everyone's journey in life.
For some people, it's a way to get from one place
to another.
For others, it's a search for one's purpose in
existence.
For me, the road was where I could find peace.
When everything in my life had shattered, I
turned to the road.
And that's where I met him.
Killian Lemarque.
A beautiful truck driver, and my salvation.
One month on the road together is the deal, and
when it's over, I will have hopefully figured out
what I'm going to do about my torn reality.
But sometimes the road can change everything.
One Month. One Truck. One Long Drive.

How You Get The Girl

As Hollywood's hottest actor, getting a woman in my bed is never a challenge.

Then I spotted her at a bar—she wanted a man for the night, and I jumped at the chance to fill the role. I gave her Joel Kline's best, and she smacked my pretty face.

But don't worry, that's not the end of our story.

Her brand of crazy inspired me, and I had to see her again, no matter the cost.

Now, Alessandra Rose is my lead makeup artist for the next four months.

Literally, her job is to touch me every day for the duration of filming. Sounds like a win, right?

Nope, she stops me at every hint of a flirt. I'm in uncharted waters for once.

Joel Kline's famous techniques to get the girl are failing me. It's no longer about those sexy Brazilian lips, or her fiery spirit that gives me a hard-on.

It's about making her banana pancakes after she spends the night in my home.

It's about knocking down those walls around her, claiming her as mine.

She's going to fight me, of course, unwilling to accept that it's not all an act.

But I'm not going anywhere; that's how you get the girl.

Guiding Lights

He sings of suffering. His eyes hold the pain of living in sorrow.

The moment our gaze meets recognition flares within.

We are tortured souls drifting in a sea of darkness.

He knows I have secrets that I'll never tell.

I am numb.

I am broken.

I am dirty.

I can never be the guiding light through the darkness he thinks I am.

I have forsaken my past, I rely on keeping myself shut off.

But he has secrets too, secrets that would destroy everything I have left.

I wish things were different, that maybe we could be each other's lifeline.

But destiny drags us down like an anchor.

The broken can only drift in the sea barely staying afloat.

Blinding Lights

She dances with a passion I'll never know.
Seeing her again tears me at the seams.
She was never mine.
My soul is stained with the darkness of death.
I have killed.
I have tortured.
I have lost.
Her soul is too bright for the shadows within,
and her determination to be the flame in my
heart could kill us both.
Still, I want her, I crave her.
But not even her blinding lights can fight away
the darkness threatening us both.
Eventually, everything gets snuffed out.

Weighing of the Heart

What happens when the myths of old become reality?

Thalia Alexander has lived her life in peace until her twenty-fifth birthday when she has a strange dream about a man.

A tall, dark, and sexy man that shows up at her work the next morning.

Tristan Jacks is trouble with a capital T, but for some strange reason she is drawn to him like nothing she has ever experienced before. He has this possessiveness and adoration for her that she can't explain. It's like they have known each other forever.

Thalia's strange dreams continue to stalk her as her relationship with Tristan builds to be a love that will last the ages.

And when those dreams and reality start to clash, will Thalia be able to handle the truth?

Could the world of ancient myths truly exist in modern times?

Evergreen

It was supposed to be an easy stakeout.
Until a bunch of bachelorettes mobbed me,
changing my life forever.

I couldn't get Andi Slaton, with her red hair, blue
eyes, and cotton candy-flavored lip gloss, out of
my head.

But when she offers herself to aid the FBI to help
me take down the biggest criminal family in
Tampa, Florida, my very sanity is put to the test
watching her spend time with my arch enemy.

She's everything I want, I will be everything to
her.
We will be Evergreen.

Playlist

Nobody Knows- The Lumineers

Unstoppable- The Score

As Real As You And Me- Rihanna

Breathe Into Me- Marian Hill

Dancing in the Dark- Rihanna

Underneath- Cobi

Cannonball- Kiesza

Gravity- John Mayer

Little Do You Know- Alex & Sierra

Broken- Lifehouse

When the Darkness Comes- Colbie Caillat

The Parting Glass- Ed Sheeran version

I found- Amber Run

Heroes- Zayde Wolf

ACKNOWEDGEMENTS

Goodness.. where do I begin.

Night is has finally come guys!

It came and now it's over.

So, so many people went into this series.

From my cousin Christina who let me tell her all about this epic tale I was going to plot. An epic superhero story.

To Leina, my friend and superhero guru who listened to all my thoughts and ideas, helping me understand the superhero ways.

To my amazing betas! Melissa Ann, MA Scott, Autumn, Marissa, Sarah, and Krystal. I COULD NOT HAVE DONE THESE BOOK WITHOUT YOU ALL. YOU HELPED PUSH ME!

Kristen (K-mazz) I'm so thankful for you. I wouldn't have made it past Dusk if it wasn't for you. Thank you <3

Amelia.. You have been pushing me and keeping my head above water since you let me be your new bestie. Forever yours biggest fan and friend.

Big BIG thank you to all the amazing Bookstagrammers and bloggers that gave my heroes a chance. I still can't believe that you picked my books. Even just sharing or something that seems so simple is huge in my eyes. Thank you so much.

My fairies were there for me every step of the way. Thank you guys for being a part of my amazing reader group. <3

My cover goddess deserves a round of applause for these covers. Night was always my favorite, and you made the vision of the epic superheroes come true with these covers.

Kiezha... girl. What would I do without you as my editor.. really? I'd fall apart!

Judy! My proofreader! You complete me and help turn my babies into masterpieces. You're the cherry on top of my team.

Emily, and the social butterfly team are amazing PR. You believed in me and have gone above and beyond what I expected. Thank you for being there.

Now to you! You who are reading this book! It's hard to put in words what you mean to me. You chose me. You gave my heroes a chance. From book one with Draco and Rose all the way to the end. I could cry. I will cry. This series has meant soo much to me, and you were willing to give it a shot. Even if you hated it I am more than thankful for that chance. Thank you soooo much!

TO my hubs and baby. I love you both.

Evee bear. I hope these books show you that you can do anything with that wild imagination of yours. That you can be your own superhero.

Asshole love of mine(HUBS) .. I love you. Thank you for believing in me too.

Sorry if typing at night kept your awake. You're a good husband for letting me write in bed. lol

Printed in Great Britain
by Amazon

57894478R00169